SPY IN CAMERA

Disillusioned with life in the South of France, Hurford accepts an assignment for British Intelligence. He is told that, under cover of a teaching post in Moscow, he will simply be expected to relay information back to Britain from a highly-prized source. In Moscow, however, Hurford finds himself involved in a complicated chain of events. The outcome for him is a mental and physical ordeal too harrowing for any man to endure.

Books by Richard Grayson
in the Linford Mystery Library:

THE MONTMARTRE MURDERS
THE DEATH OF ABBÉ DIDIER

RICHARD GRAYSON

SPY IN CAMERA

Complete and Unabridged

LINFORD
Leicester

First published in Great Britain

First Linford Edition
published 1997

British Library CIP Data

Grayson, Richard
Spy in camera.—Large print ed.—
Linford mystery library
1. Detective and mystery stories
2. Large type books
I. Title
823.9′14 [F]

ISBN 0–7089–5096–5

Published by
F. A. Thorpe (Publishing) Ltd.
Anstey, Leicestershire

Set by Words & Graphics Ltd.
Anstey, Leicestershire
Printed and bound in Great Britain by
T. J. International Ltd., Padstow, Cornwall

This book is printed on acid-free paper

Part One

Focus

1

THE first thing Hurford saw when his eyes opened was a fly on Nicole's bare shoulders. He lay there, wondering why he had woken so abruptly, switching from insensibility to daylight in one startling instant. Twenty years before he had often woken like that, in a mountain hut or a cave, sensing danger but finding only the frozen brightness of the night and the rough breath of the others. Since then idleness and soft living had induced a different sort of daybreak; slow and reluctant and enervating.

Sunlight, piercing the stale warmth of the bedroom, fell across Nicole's back and the long strands of her dark hair. Her skin was brown and coarsened by too much exposure on the beach. Spotlighted, the fly was rubbing its front legs together. Hurford remembered peasant women washing clothes on the rocks by streams outside their villages.

Kicking the sheet away, he swung his legs over the bed. There was no danger of waking Nicole. He could tell from her breathing and from the way she lay slumped in the bed that she was sleeping at her heaviest. The sheet, falling away, revealed her bare back down to the cleft where her heavy buttocks began. It was hard to believe that she was still only twenty-three. Her hips were the hips of a matron even though her face was a girl's.

The thought of girls reminded him of his interview with Monsieur Jaillot, the headmaster of the school where, until eight days ago, he had taught. Incredulity and anger at Jaillot's accusations had passed and given place to brooding resentment.

He walked naked into the living room. Through the window one could glimpse, past the pink walls of the house opposite, a corner of the harbour and the bay beyond. A yacht which had not been there the night before lay at anchor in the bay. Large and white and pretentious, it dwarfed the cruisers and the launches of the vedettes and racehorse owners, a tribute to hellenic opportunism.

The girl who had been the subject of Jaillot's charges he could scarcely even remember. Suzanne? Brigitte? Françoise? A thin girl with large eyes and, one would have supposed, utterly without sex. Her father, an official in an obscure government department, had laid the complaint.

He shaved and dressed slowly, deliberating whether to put on slacks and sweater or his working suit. What would Savage wear? He remembered him as clever and perceptive; as a man who was careful to observe the conventions even though he always mocked himself for doing so. Hurford chose the suit and looked rather self-consciously in a drawer for his regimental tie. Why not? He would certainly have worn it if he had been going to be interviewed for a job, which in one sense he was.

Leaving the apartment without waking Nicole, he walked down the steep lane to the harbour and from there to the Croisette. At a café near the Carlton he drank a coffee and smoked his first cigarette.

The fact that he had met Savage by chance in a bar, at a time when he needed a job, did not surprise him. All his life he had held a Micawberish belief in providence. Luck, coincidence, fate, whatever one cared to call it, invariably came to his aid in his not infrequent moments of crisis.

There was an hour to waste before he was to meet Savage in the bar of the Martinez. He walked along the Croisette between the palm trees and the sea. It was still early and the beach was empty except for a few fanatics. A shrivelled Frenchwoman, approaching sixty, lay on a purple and yellow towel, stroking the arm of her companion. He was perhaps fifteen years younger than she, lean and hollow-chested. "Ah, mon chou," Hurford heard the woman's insinuating voice. "You must hurry and bronze yourself. You are so handsome when you are bronzed!"

He thought, God, the French could make a sexual situation out of a couple of dead twigs. He had lived in Cannes for four years, imitated their life, adopted their tongue and yet had never ceased inwardly to despise the French.

He walked along by the sea slowly for perhaps a mile and then back. When he reached the Martinez, there were still four minutes remaining before his rendezvous, but he went through the hotel lobby and into the bar. Without thinking he asked for a Vin Blanc Cassis and then changed his order to a Scotch.

It had been in the bar of the Martinez that he had met Nicole, only a few weeks after he had come

7

to live in Cannes. He had gone there, he remembered, looking for sex and a Greek girl named Maria who, people had told him, was a pushover, an amateur. Nicole had been drinking with an elderly American artist. She had gone back to Hurford's apartment that night and stayed there ever since. She had told him she worked as an assistant in a chemist's shop, but he found out later that she had been out of work for a fortnight. They never went back to the Martinez now, but did their drinking in the cheaper cafés near the harbour.

Savage came in and immediately took away what Hurford had thought would be a psychological advantage by saying: "Drink up and let's go outside. This is my only holiday of the year and I need all the sun I can get."

He was wearing an unbelievably dirty pair of brown linen slacks and a blue towelling shirt with a triangular tear in one shoulder. They sat on the terrace outside the hotel and drank Vin Blanc Cassis.

Savage said: "It's all fixed. I spoke with my contact in London by telephone last night and the job is yours if you want it. There would have to be an interview in London but that's just a formality; wool to pull over the eyes of the taxpayer."

"No references needed?"

"We'll put a tame scriptwriter on to that. Your record is the only reference we need." He looked at Hurford and smiled. The smile could have been an apology but it was either masked by cynicism or could not suppress it. "You're intelligent enough to have realised that it's not a straight teaching job."

"If it was, you could have found a thousand people better qualified than me."

"You'd be working for intelligence. Nothing very dramatic, I'm afraid. Not even espionage in the real sense. We need a courier in Moscow. Someone to collect information from one of our best agents and ship it home to us."

Hurford stared through the trees that bordered the Croisette at the sea. A man in pale green trunks was water-skiing, following a motor-boat in a sweeping turn. His nonchalance was disdainful and professional. One could almost smell the Ambre Solaire on his muscled back, see the grey hairs at his temple which the black rinse could not conceal.

"What's the expectancy of this job?" Hurford asked and then corrected himself. "No, I'm not thinking in terms of danger. I mean how long am I likely to be in Russia?"

"The normal tour at the Institute is three years, but I would think we'd have to pull you out before then."

"And afterwards?"

"We can't give you any guarantees, but if it was at all possible we'd certainly use you somewhere else. Teaching is a good cover, you know."

If he only went for two years,

Hurford reflected, he might be able to work out something with Nicole; send her enough money to keep on the apartment. Even as the thought struck him, he wondered why he could not help applying British middle-class principles to a situation that was wholly French. No one would expect him to do the right thing by the girl, least of all Nicole herself.

They finished their drinks without discussing the proposition any further. Hurford knew the form. Details of a job like the one for which Savage was recruiting him were not settled over drinks on an hotel terrace. Besides, what else did he need to know? He was a few years out of touch on pay rates but the rest of the routine had probably not changed much.

It was nearing midday. The rich who could afford to waste five hours of daylight in bed and the debauched who needed to, were rousing themselves and shuffling across the road from their hotels to the beach. A young

11

girl with long fair hair, who wore a cap tilted over her eyes, crossed the forecourt of the Martinez. In her bikini she looked frighteningly thin. Hurford tried to picture her lying in bed beside him and the idea seemed not so much unreal as indecent.

"Bum like a choirboy." Savage's eyes were following the girl as well. His choice of a word that dated back long before the officers' mess to juvenile vulgarity seemed grotesque. "They could use her in an Oxfam ad.," he added.

"Have the other half?"

"Some other time. I want my swim first."

"When must I let you know?"

"It's fairly urgent. Till we get someone to Moscow we're wasting a damn good source, one of the best we've ever had in fact."

"I'll phone you this evening."

"Fine! Not before six, though. I'll be on the beach till six."

When Hurford arrived back at the

apartment, Nicole was awake, sitting on the edge of the bed and combing her hair. She wore only his old silk dressing-gown, tightly tied round her waist but loose everywhere else. Her bare feet were large and looked somehow flat, like the pads of a heavy animal.

"Make me some coffee, Mike," she said and smiled. He sensed that she was in one of these extremely amiable moods that had been rare for the past year or so.

He heated some of the coffee that remained from the previous evening and brought it to her in the bedroom. She was still sitting on the bed, staring ahead of her, absolutely motionless. He could feel in her stillness that blend of complete repose and expectancy which never failed to move him. When, handing her the coffee, he leant forward, he could see her breasts. He caught a strand of her hair and tugged at it gently.

"Wait till I've drunk my coffee,"

she said without any emotion, without smiling.

Hurford sat on the bed beside her, fighting back the sudden urgency, trying to match her tranquillity. Finally she stopped drinking, put her cup down and then twisted suddenly, pushing him back on the bed.

Her love-making was aggressive and commanding. Usually he would have accepted it almost passively, but today she triggered off an equal savagery inside him. In a single instant of floodlit clarity before the downward vortex of passion, he realised it was because he knew this would be the last time.

Afterwards he sat and watched her at the dressing table as she put up her hair.

"I've been offered a job," he said at last.

"By your English friend?" Her intuition surprised him. He had mentioned his first meeting with Savage but nothing more.

"It's a teaching post in Russia."

"I don't wish to go to Russia."

"Why not? You know nothing about the country."

From this starting point, slowly, elaborately, like two people playing a Chinese game, they built up their quarrel. They knew all each other's moves, but this did not make the exchanges any less intense. Sarcasm was replaced by bitterness, bitterness by clumsy anger.

"Go back to your regiment!" she hissed at him. "Go back and enjoy your schoolboy games. Play at being a British officer again. What does it matter if you're middle-aged?"

"I've already told you it's a teaching job. Are you stupid?"

"Past forty and already inadequate." She did not know his age but had to taunt him where a Frenchman would have been most vulnerable.

"You're right. I should have sense enough to know I'm too old to satisfy a waterfront nymphomaniac."

15

"And what do you hope to find in Russia? Some whore as middle-aged as yourself?"

"My self-respect perhaps." He knew he sounded pompous and British and all the other things she affected to despise and the knowledge made him even angrier.

"Oh, foutez . . ."

He looked at her, wondering how long ago his disillusionment in her and the life they led had began.

2

THE canvas was undated, but immediately recognisable as an early Heike. An abstract built up on a diagonal axis, cobalt and mauve predominated, as they so often had in the painter's work during his Nordic period.

Bartle had been gazing at it for several minutes, satisfied now that the painting was hung in a manner consistent with its excellence — and its price. Eight thousand seven hundred and fifty new francs. The fact that his friends would assume, as they were supposed to, that it was a copy, only added in some perverted way to his pride of possession. He remembered the subterfuges he had invented, the precautions he had taken to conceal his identity when it had been bought, for cash of course, from the gallery in the Rue du Faubourg St. Honoré. His only regret was that he could not risk refurnishing his flat to provide a setting worthy of the Heike. Even so, there could be other pictures and perhaps a genuine antique or two, if he was discreet. He sat down at the horrid little walnut bureau from Tottenham Court Road, took a sheet of paper and began earning the money that could pay for them.

The list which he had to compile each week was a long one, but he had an exceptionally retentive memory and never needed to keep notes, which reduced the security risk. Thirty-seven items had been ordered during the week for the Ministry of Defence research unit in Dorset. Chemicals, optical and laboratory equipment, even office furniture; he listed them all, with quantities or dimensions in every case. He had long ago ceased to wonder how the list could be of value to a foreign power and now no longer believed that it was. The whole operation was a piece of organised stupidity, intelligence for the sake of intelligence, to satisfy some bureaucrat in a Moscow office. As an order clerk in the supply department of the Ministry, he was prepared to accept that other countries might also have Civil Servants who created work to justify promotion, another assistant, a bigger samovar.

When the list was finished he pulled out the copy of *Little Dorrit* from the bookcase. Why were the Russians obsessed with Dickens? Because they were eighty years out-of-date in their culture or because it suited them politically to pretend that the life Dickens portrayed was typical of Britain today? The fact that he could despise the people for whom he worked was comforting.

The day was the fourteenth of the month. He subtracted fourteen from thirty-one, turned to page seventeen and began coding the list. As a security precaution, its futility amused him, but the actual work, the orderly transfer of letters to cyphers, gave him satisfaction.

When he had finished it was almost time for his rendezvous with Donaldson. This week it would be at the Admiral Codrington. As he left the room, he glanced once more at the Heike, savouring the pleasure that it gave him and which was worth, he knew now, all the humiliation he had endured.

The Admiral Codrington was full of young men in chukka boots and girls whose thighs were too fat for mini-skirts. A middle-aged rake who had tried to stay young by having his hair styled, was chatting up his girl friend.

He said urgently: "Can't we go back to your place for a quickie?"

"No question, sweetie. Carl will be home any moment."

"We could borrow Peter's flat."

"Borrow? At a fiver an hour? It's extortion!"

"Come on, darling. Just because your husband's a Jew, you don't have to be mean about money."

"Why not? I'd be paying, wouldn't

I? Or has your wife increased your pocket-money?"

The door opened and Donaldson came into the bar. Bartle bought him a pint of bitter and ordered himself another Bourbon. He was slowly growing accustomed to the sour taste of Bourbon, which he had only taken to drinking since he'd discovered it was the tipple of wealthy, American queers.

"You shouldn't drink spirits all the time," said Donaldson, thinking no doubt of security.

"I simply loathe the taste of beer. Horrid!"

"You could try cider."

Every time Donaldson lifted his glass, Bartle could see up his sleeve almost to the forearm. The black hairs above his wrist were profuse and thick.

"Well?" Donaldson sounded impatient which was unlike him.

"Mandrake Gardens."

"Right. Number fourteen."

"I see."

In this way he told Donaldson that he had left this week's coded list in their Mandrake Gardens dead-letter box, the underside of a bench, to which he had secured it with adhesive tape. In return he had learnt that in three days he could collect his money from dead-letter box number fourteen which was in Gloucester Mews.

Bartle smiled to himself and thought, if he only knew that he need not have blackmailed me into working for him, there are more ways than one, much more pleasant.

Donaldson finished his beer and ordered another round of drinks. He was thinking of his wife in Minsk whom he had not seen now for eleven years. It was not with any special affection that he remembered her, but with disbelief. Try as he might, he could not accept that there was ever a time when he could have lived the kind of life which he knew they had shared. In eleven years he had moved through vast orbits of experience, built a new life and a personality for himself that was now much more real than anything he could remember from the past.

A few minutes later, when he left Bartle in the pub, he took a devious route to the mews off Brompton Road, where he had left his car. Walking to South Kensington, he took the tube to Charing Cross, a bus to Tottenham Court Road, walked from there to Oxford Circus, took a taxi to Green Park station, from where he caught the tube again, this time to Gloucester Road.

Miss Hardstaff was waiting on the corner of a drab street in Fulham and her moist smile wrapped round him as she climbed quickly into the car. His association with Miss Hardstaff filled Donaldson with distaste, even though he did not allow himself the bourgeois luxury of admitting it. She was not a plain woman and took great pains with her appearance, but her eagerness was like damp seeping through over-bright wallpaper. She squeezed his hand as it rested on the knob of the gear lever and he knew exactly what she was thinking.

When, sharing the back seat of the car on Wimbledon Common, he kissed her she laughed expectantly. "Marvellous! Give my compliments to the chef." Her contact lenses glittering in the darkness were jewels in a toad's forehead.

He did his best for the Soviet and then had to endure one of the interminable conversations which to Miss Hardstaff appeared to be a form of post-sacrificial ritual, essential to final consummation. Eventually he was rewarded with a sheaf of reports neatly clipped together. They were copies of the latest batch of tests carried out in the pathological laboratory where she worked, on specimens sent in from an establishment in Dorset. She knew that the specimens came from animals and that the tests always revealed some remarkable deviations from the normal which suggested exposure to unlikely bacteria. She did not wish to know anything more.

Donaldson drove her back to Fulham, dropping her in a different street, and then took the car back to the mews. From an all-night garage a few minutes away, he picked up another car which he owned and drove back in it to his flat at Holland Park, stopping for a few moments at Mandrake Gardens.

His precautions were unnecessary, for he was not being followed. But he had not even noticed in the Admiral Codrington a man with a deaf aid who sat across the room. Nor was he to know that before he had arrived a young woman had gone up to the bar alongside Bartle on the pretext of buying cigarettes and had stayed there long enough to fix a tiny microphone under the bar counter with chewing gum. Before he reached the dead-letter box in Mandrake Gardens, Bartle's list had been taken out, photographed and replaced. And the couple entwined in a nearby Mini when he parked his first car after returning from his meeting with Miss Hardstaff were Sergeant Dace of the Special Branch and a woman constable. Ten minutes after he had left, Sergeant Dace walked over to Donaldson's car, opened the door with a key and took away a small tape recorder which had been concealed earlier that evening under the driver's seat.

3

"HOW are you feeling today?"
"All right, sir. Absolutely first class!"

Zollick studied the man as they were speaking. Although the pale, drawn look still remained, his eyes were clear, the mouth firm. There was no doubt at all that Lieutenant Fisher was a great deal nearer normal health, mental as well as physical, than he had been only two weeks previously. To confirm what his observations told him, he gave Fisher an exhaustive examination. "What do you plan to do when we release you?" he asked as he checked Fisher's reflexes.

"The colonel said I would have a month's leave, sir."

"You deserve it."

Fisher hesitated. "Unless of course you'd need me back here sooner."

Zollick saw the anxiety and understood. "No. All our tests are over. We would like you to report back at the end of your leave for another check. Just to reassure ourselves. But in the meantime go and enjoy yourself. Take a couple of weeks abroad if you can."

Lieutenant Fisher's laugh was full of relief and satisfaction. Volunteering for this business would be a worthwhile mention in his records, but he was glad to know it was over. As he was dressing, Ashby, the resident doctor at the nursing home, came into the room.

"Will that be all, sir?"

"Yes. See the matron about the papers for your discharge and you can leave tomorrow."

"Thank you, sir."

"We should be thanking you. Good luck."

Ashby waited until Fisher had left the room. Then, as he made an entry in a case history sheet on the desk, he asked Zollick: "How did he strike you?"

"Excellent. There's nothing wrong with Lieutenant Fisher."

"The others were all the same. It's remarkable really. As though the smears on a mirror had just been wiped away."

"That's not a bad analogy. Still, one must not read too much into these results."

"You're still not satisfied?"

Zollick shook his head. With his sharp nose and tonsure of white hair above a long neck, he looked like an ostrich.

"It isn't like that. But we can only assess the value of this new drug on its performance so far. How have we used it? On three groups of volunteer patients. Admittedly they all had some history of neurotic disturbance and we subjected them artificially to as much stress as possible. But all this is no substitute for the real thing."

"We also gave them the same injections as we know our friends behind the Iron Curtain use on their victims."

"Yes, but in entirely different circumstances."

"What else could we do?"

"Very little, I admit. But we still don't know whether the drugs will have the same effect on a man when the Russians have finished with him. I would like to have made more tests, if there was time."

"You don't think there is?"

"No. I'm being pressed very hard from the highest levels."

Zollick put on his Homburg and stuffed papers into his breast-pocket. Outside the nursing home his chauffeur opened the door of the Bentley for him. As the car swung through the gates and headed towards Hampstead, a plain clothes officer standing in the drive raised his hand in a salute.

4

HURFORD walked along Carnaby Street, threading his way through the tourists who were staring into the shops and trying to spot the queers. In his ten-year-old blue serge and military style topcoat he felt like a fossil; a relic of those brave old days that everyone now despised. Even though he had abandoned England, it angered him to find London a peep-show for sardonic Frenchmen and supercilious, well-dressed Teutons. He would have liked a drink, but it seemed wrong to arrive for a medical examination with the smell of alcohol on his breath.

The Selection Board with whom he had spent forty-five minutes in courteous conversation, had appeared suitably impressed with his qualifications: scholar of Peterhouse, first in Modern Languages, fluent in French, German,

Italian, passable in Spanish, Serbo-Croat and Russian. His army record, too, had commanded their nodding approval. Only one old woman on the Board had shown passing doubts. He thought of her as old, but she had probably been no more than sixty: a superannuated Liberal politician and social worker, prematurely wrinkled by the exhaustion of trying to force her admirable beliefs on a reluctant society.

She had asked Hurford, peevishly, why he had spent the last four years teaching in, of all places, a French girls' school. There were several evasive answers he could have given and he chose what he thought would be the most acceptable.

"After I left the Army my marriage broke up. I'm afraid I didn't take it very well. I wanted to get away from everything and France seemed a good place." Even as he spoke he realised that he was by implication putting the blame on Margery, which was scarcely the behaviour of an officer. But his answer achieved the right effect. From behind the spectacles opposite a beam of maidenish sympathy shone out at him, bright and forgiving.

The Board had accepted him because they had to. Instructions had been passed down, unwritten but unambiguous, from echelons of the Establishment above their knowing. It had probably made it easier for their consciences to believe he was suitable for the post.

Now, in Regent Street, two girls in mini-skirts passed him and the sight of their thighs thrust a shaft of nostalgic lust for Nicole into him. He wondered what one did about sex in London now that they had driven the girls off the streets. The clip joints in Soho, as *Paris Match* had exposed, were only good for blackcurrant cordial and false pretences. In France there would have been no problem. Once more he felt the depressing sense of being a stranger in his home.

He walked slowly to Harley Street,

where the doctor's receptionist made him fill in a medical history sheet while he waited. The answers to the questions came automatically but they no longer held any meaning. Date of birth, parents' age at decease, childhood illnesses, history of insanity, epilepsy, tuberculosis; once they all must at least have brought pictures to the mind. Now they were a litany of his unbelief in life.

The doctor tested his blood pressure, heart, reflexes, hearing, vision and urine. Then he began asking a long series of personal questions, which were factual at first but became gradually more subjective.

"What sort of lasting effect has war, do you think, on a man's personality? . . . And how would you describe the symptoms? . . . Can you give me an example? . . . And does this coincide with your own experience?"

The questioning veered to more personal matters, to his marriage and his relationship with Margery.

"My wife wouldn't give me a divorce," Hurford said and realised that the lie of convenience which he had invented as a defence — unnecessary as it proved — against Nicole, was now more real for him than the truth.

The doctor phrased his questions with discretion but his probing delicacy was as incisive as a lancet. It was a relief when he returned to medical matters. How much alcohol did Hurford consume in an average day? Cigarettes? Finally a visit to the scales and a check on his height.

While the receptionist was showing Hurford out, the doctor made notes on his observations and attached them to the complete medical sheet. He wrote quickly, without pausing for thought, as though he were entirely confident in his judgement.

When he had finished the report he picked up the telephone and asked his receptionist to get him a Whitehall number. After a long wait, while anonymous people were going through the routines of security, he heard Savage reply.

He told him: "Your chap Hurford just left me."

"What's your opinion?"

"For what you have in mind, I would say he was ideally suited."

"That's grand!" Savage's tone was full of satisfaction, as though now some lingering doubt had been dispelled. "That's all we needed to get the go ahead. Thanks very much, Zollick."

5

IN an office near Westminster, Sergeant Dace was typing a detailed report on Donaldson's meeting with Bartle in the Admiral Codrington. When complete, it would be delivered in a sealed packet together with the tape from the recorder hidden in Donaldson's car, to Colonel Fenton. The report had to be personally typed, with no carbons. Sergeant Boxhall, who shared the office with Dace, was typing a not dissimilar report on the members of an espionage cell that centred on a Principal in the Foreign Office.

"I wonder what a ghost-writer gets paid," Dace remarked and when Boxhall only grunted, he explained: "I might as well be writing this rogue's autobiography."

"What have you got to moan about? I've been on my job for

nine weeks now."

"But have you got anything on them that would stand up to the Old Bailey?"

"There's enough in my reports to put my friend and his whole circus away for nine lives each. Short of stripping the P.M.'s files bare, he could hardly've got in deeper."

Dace pulled the last sheet of his report out of the machine, read it through, signed it and clipped it with the other four pages. Like many policemen, although he complained about paperwork, he secretly enjoyed preparing reports. To recount the events in an orderly sequence, without elaboration, was satisfying, marking as this did another stage in the methodical progression of an assignment.

He said to Boxhall: "Doesn't it strike you as being irregular?"

"Irregular?"

"Unusual then. Between the two of us we've collected enough evidence to convict half-a-dozen people and still no one makes a move to pull them in."

"Yes. And I know for a fact that there are at least another four cases in London, let alone the provinces."

Dace lit a cigarette and began the routine procedure of sealing his report and the tape in a maximum security container. He had always smoked too much, even in the days before he was seconded from the Metropolitan Police and played open-side wing forward every Saturday at Imber Court. Otherwise he might have had more than one trial for Middlesex.

"No doubt about it," he observed. "Something pretty outsize is being kept hidden under somebody's bowler."

"Sure. And the first you and I will know about it is when some port-nosed Q.C. begins to cross-examine us in the witness box."

6

"IT is estimated that every week in summer more than one million Russians from outside Moscow pass through the capital. Special tourist hotels offering low-priced accommodation exist specially for these visitors."

The voice on the tape machine continued reciting monotonously in excellent Russian the catalogue of attractions and civic achievements in Moscow. Alone in the sound-proof booth at the language laboratory, Hurford wondered why the British Institute should use stereotyped Russian propaganda as training material. His job when he reached Moscow was supposed to be teaching Russians about the British way of life.

The refresher course in the language was to last two weeks, studying nine hours a day. Already after four days his familiarity with Russian had returned and he was moving towards a fluency that he had never acquired under the tuition of émigrés at Cambridge.

The tape continued to unwind, dispensing its programmed knowledge with transistorised efficiency. Hurford found his attention wandering. His thoughts turned again to Nicole. At this time of the morning she would just about have surfaced and might be going out for the first drink. He could visualise her ungraceful walk, her clothes; the orange blouse, the blue jeans that were too light across her hips, with a crudely mended slit to remind him of an evening when eagerness had made him clumsy. She would walk through the narrow streets till she reached the first mean bar that took her fancy. She might even be accompanied. By now some other man, more capable than him if no more fastidious, could have moved in to share the apartment. The thought that as they walked the man's hand would be resting on her hips, gave Hurford a twinge of jealousy.

Irritated at his own weakness, he forced his mind back to his work. "With its broad streets and classical architecture, Moscow provides an outstanding example of the town planner's art."

What the hell was this supposed to be? Teaching or brainwashing?

Suddenly there was a break in the recording. The Russian monologue stopped abruptly to be followed by a moment's silence. Then an English voice began.

"These are the instructions you are to follow after your arrival in Moscow. The first three weeks you will spend getting established in your normal routine work at the British Institute. You will not be given any special treatment at the Institute, nor should you expect any. No one in the Institute knows your real function. The same is true of the Embassy, with the exception of the three people there who will be your contacts. Under no circumstances

42

will you discuss any aspect of your work with these contacts, nor are you to go to them in emergencies. On certain occasions you will use these Embassy officials as a post office to relay information through the diplomatic bag back to us, but nothing more."

The voice was that of Savage. Hurford smiled. It was wholly in character for the man to choose this melodramatic way of passing information. Even in their army days Savage had always been attracted by the bizarre and the secretive, the whisper behind the hand.

"When eventually we decide that you are ready to start operations, you will receive a ticket for the Bolshoi theatre by letter. During the first interval of the performance you will leave your seat to have a drink or a smoke or merely for fresh air. Sometime during the evening information will be passed to you which you will take home and pass, at an opportune moment, to the Cultural Attaché. Thereafter you will receive instructions by coded telephone calls and other methods. These methods will all be explained in your next session at the language laboratory and you will memorise them. In the meantime you are to play through this portion of the tape and erase the recording. That is all."

There was a pause and then the Russian voice picked up its commentary, coming in on a broken word, which showed that Savage's message had been cut into the original recording. Hurford played the instructions through once more and then erased them, checking to ensure that every word had been removed. A painstaking concern with details, particularly in the matter of cover and security, was, he knew, essential to successful intelligence work. He was pleased to find that the habits inculcated by his earlier training remained, even after so many years of inactivity.

In spite of Nicole's sneers he was not too old for work that demanded discipline and persistence.

7

Report Form 671 A
    Priority Classification — Routine

Destination Komitet Gosudarstvennoi
              Bezopasnosti European
              Directorate, Central
              Headquarters, Moscow
Sender   Security Officer, Visa
              Section, U.S.S.R.
              Embassy, London.
Subject   Visa Application — British
              Subject

Application received from MICHAEL
CLIVE FREESTONE HURFORD, appointed
Senior Assistant Lecturer, British
Institute Moscow. Age: forty-three.
Education: Chesterfield Grammar
School, Peterhouse College, Cambridge.
Marital status: separated. Served with
British Army as artillery officer and

45

later in Intelligence Corps 1943 – 6
Granted permanent commission after
end of war. Resigned 1960. Civilian
work: publishing, B.B.C. journalism,
teaching. Political affiliations: nothing
known.

Proposed entry to U.S.S.R.   15/6
Period of stay   3 years
Visa granted effect from

Message Form 23
              Priority Classification — 3

Destination Security Officer, Visa
              Section, U.S.S.R.
              Embassy, London.
Sender   European Directorate, Cen-
              tral Headquarters, K.G.B.

Reference report Michael Clive
Freestone Hurford. Further information
required concerning applicant, in
particular military record and subsequent employment. Full enquiries
should be instituted.

8

IN spite of Savage's pretence that he was a light-hearted dilettante, Hurford had always thought of him as a highly professional intelligence operator. So when he reported at the office in Cork Street which was the Equipment Section of the department, he was appalled at its whimsical amateurism.

Fossick, head of the Section, was a museum-piece of the 1950's. He lived in Chislehurst, supported the Liberal Party and took exercise conscientiously every Saturday afternoon at a tennis club, where he made up for his appalling lack of athleticism by buying more than his fair share of drinks at the bar.

"Going operational? Lucky you! Don't know why I say that, though, because I've never had the guts. Born for the

47

backroom. One of nature's egg-heads."

"I'm not sure I'll be any good," Hurford said. "Things were different in the war."

"Ah! Gallantry. Parachuted into Europe, I'll bet." Hurford nodded, so Fossick went on: "Shivers! Nothing partisan about me. Strictly neutral. Not neuter though, ask the wife, she can show you three reasons why not." He enjoyed his joke, grinning and pulling his collar away from his neck with one finger, so he could waggle his chin in comfort.

"What have you got for me?" Hurford asked, controlling his impatience.

"Nothing much. We don't send sophisticated gadgets into Russia. They'll search your luggage anyway."

Fossick went to a metal cupboard and took out a cardboard box which he placed on the table. From the box he lifted out a camera, a pair of binoculars and a portable radio. All three looked worn and shabby.

"Positively Bulldog Drummond. But

they are all that you'll need."

"Perhaps things aren't so different after all," Hurford remarked.

"Oh, we've piles of modern stuff. Toothpick microphones, bleepers. But not for you. Can't even show them to you. Don't want the Russians to know about our equipment."

"Does that mean you think I'll tell them?"

"Humorist! Writer of Hancock scripts? No? You'll agree we must allow for all possibilities. What if you were arrested?"

Fossick picked up the binoculars. He explained that they were fitted with special lenses and could be used for reading signals in infra-red light, which would not be visible to the naked eye. The radio set had a concealed switch by which it could be tuned to a special short-wave frequency for transmissions from Britain.

"What about the camera?"

"Just a camera. Part-worn tourist equipment. Not so clever these Japanese, after all. But good cover, as you'll find out."

"And is this all I take?"

"Hysterics! Traumatic!" Fossick, his wife and their intelligent middle-class friends always conversed in a sort of private shorthand, where single words did the work of whole sentences. They had cultivated it unconsciously as a form of defence. Using this group language, they could be witty with each other yet not embarrass outsiders by a show of intellect. "Didn't I tell you your luggage will be searched? You just take the camera. Shoulder slung. Issue for tourist troops."

"And the radio and binoculars."

"Special delivery. Fortnum's little horse van. You'll find them in your apartment when you get there."

He packed the cardboard box up again carefully, leaving the camera on the table. It could be slipped, case and all, into Hurford's briefcase when he left the Section.

"There you are. Nothing to it. Didn't

hurt after all, did it?"

Hurford replied gravely: "Hysterical. Traumatic."

Fossick grinned, interpreting this as a compliment. "You're getting the idea."

9

CROWDS had gathered in the gardens outside the Bolshoi theatre as they always do on warm June evenings. Men in open-necked shirts, accompanied by chunky women in dowdy cotton dresses; flat, grey faces, lustreless after years of monotonous existence and a diet of carbohydrates, stared at the fountains or the traffic or other people. Slow, unemotional, slugs around a cabbage. A few hung hopefully around the entrance to the theatre. On rare occasions it had been known for a ticket to become available.

Hurford mingled with the crowds, hoping subconsciously perhaps that his tension might be absorbed by their insensibility and so be concealed. He had been in Moscow for three uneventful weeks. Every day he lectured earnest adult students for two or three hours on the English language and British institutions. He had helped to organise open discussions, a conversazione, debates, a mock trial and an English thé dansant. In his ample leisure, to relieve the growing boredom and impatience, he had been on guided tours of the city to the Ostankina Palace, the Exhibition of Economic Achievement, the University, workers' flats, schools, hospitals, crêches. The sheer monolithic achievement of it all, the inhumanity of regimented welfare, oppressed him.

Then, that morning, the ticket for the Bolshoi had arrived. It had come, anonymously and without comment, in an unstamped envelope that he had found in his pigeonhole at the Institute's staff room. Two or three seconds had passed before he remembered Savage's instructions and realised its significance. The knowledge had brought not fear but excitement and a feeling almost of elation that at last the waiting was over.

The seat was for the evening performance of two ballets: *Coppelia* and a modern piece that was new to him. He had walked from the Institute to the theatre, making a detour through the Alexandrovosky Gardens and past the History Museum. In this way he had arrived with only a couple of minutes to waste. Now as the tourists and party workers lucky enough to have tickets filed into the Bolshoi, he followed them.

Inside, the theatre, with its over-ornate décor, was uncomfortably hot. The start of *Coppelia* was delayed for twenty minutes, to await the arrival of the Secretary of the Central Communist Party Committee and his guests, two politicians from Indonesia. When they arrived the audience stood to applaud them and Hurford felt he must do the same. The Indonesians in their three-hundred-dollar American suits smiled ivory smiles. Gold and diamonds sparkled richly among their fingers as they clapped themselves.

Coppelia was beautifully danced but, it seemed to Hurford, lacked emotion. As an undergraduate he had been enthusiastic about ballet, to the point of joining the University Ballet Club. Now he found it difficult to believe that he could ever have entertained young ladies from a visiting ballet company in his rooms with vodka and caviar and talked knowledgeably about entrechats and elevation.

After seven curtain calls, nobly sustained by the professional claque, the audience surged out for the interval. Remembering Savage's instructions he went with them and fought his way through to the refreshment bar in time to get a coffee. As he drank it, he wondered how and when his contact would pass him the information Savage had mentioned. Perhaps there had been a hitch. The contact might know that they were both under surveillance and in this case would make no move. Hurford had no experience of intelligence operations under peacetime conditions and the uncertainty was making him restless.

He was a few seconds late returning to the auditorium and the curtain was rising as he passed down the row to his seat. In the dim light he did not see the programme that lay on his seat. Feeling it beneath him when he sat down, his first impulse was to pull it out and offer it to his neighbours, one of whom must have dropped it there. His own programme was in his pocket. Then an idea exploded. Of course, he thought, and bloody fool that you are, you nearly foozled it, gave the game away.

For twenty minutes he sat watching the ballet. Then, cautiously, he pulled the programme out and opened it, pretending to search for the name of one of the ballerinas. He could just make out the lines of scribbled handwriting down the length of one margin. For several minutes he held the programme closed in front of him and then slipped it casually into his breast-pocket.

The ballet he was watching was a theatrical piece, full of melodrama, acted against a spectacular backcloth of skyscraper buildings with virtuoso lighting effects, each of which the audience applauded wildly. The storyline was heavy with political innuendo, a parable of workers in a Western city, which could only have been New York, oppressed by capitalist bosses. A tenuous love story twisted its way through the shafts of propaganda.

The claque led the way to ten curtain calls this time, after which the audience inched its way through the aisles into the night. Hurford would have liked to leave while the applause continued, but he was afraid in case he drew attention to himself.

He took the Metro to Komsomol-skaya and then walked down Sadovaya Samatechnaya to the sandstone building where the junior staff of the British Embassy and the Institute were housed together. A uniformed policeman stood on guard in a sentry-box outside, ostensibly to protect the inhabitants of the diplomatic ghetto from anti-Western demonstrations by the crowds.

Inside his apartment he was careful to bolt the door before taking the Bolshoi programme from his pocket The message which he found written on one of the inside pages was disappointing. It consisted simply of a list of names, against each of which was an address in Britain. Neither the names — Hardy, Godfrey, Manners, Donaldson, nor the addresses in London, Birmingham, Glasgow, and Cardiff, meant anything to him.

He reminded himself that he was only a courier, a passer-on of the pearls which others had dredged from dangerous depths. The less he knew about the goods in which he had to traffic, the better. That way he could betray no secrets, unwittingly or under pressure.

Hiding the programme among his shirts and underclothes, he treated himself to three fingers of Scotch to help him sleep and got ready for bed. Next morning he would hand it over to Dixon, the Cultural Attaché from the Embassy. The instructions had been more than clear. Dixon called daily at the Institute and during the coffee break in the staff room, Hurford would tell him about the ballets he had seen at the Bolshoi. He would give Dixon the programme to study at his leisure. Within twenty-four hours it would be on its way to London in the diplomatic bag.

There was nothing to it. Spying made easy. As he lay in bed Hurford wondered how intelligence could have been conducted in the days before air travel and globe-trotting politicians had left diplomats with nothing to do except sales promotion and espionage.

10

KITIMOV said to the man who sat facing him across his desk: "Well, what have you got for me this week?"

"Twenty-three altogether, Comrade Colonel."

"That's better. Last week you brought only fifteen. As I told you then, it is essential that I should be kept fully informed on every case in which material investigations are being conducted. There is a growing tendency among the Heads of Directorates to take too much responsibility on themselves."

Lermev shuffled the papers which he held in his hands impatiently. He had heard all this before. Kitimov, like many other senior Soviet officials, was obsessed with fear that his subordinates might be intriguing against him.

"First there is the Pole, Hauptman."

They began going through the typewritten reports which Lermev had brought in with him. Hauptman was a high-ranking engineer working on a vast hydro-electric project near Kazan. A few weeks earlier reports had been received that he was disseminating counter-revolutionary propaganda, that he had organised a group of malcontents into a subversive cell. Investigation had revealed no evidence except rumour and hearsay, but the Pole had been detained for interrogation. Privately Lermev believed that the accusations were false, based on nothing more than envy or malice. But the machine, once started, must grind on. In due course people would be found who could be frightened into testifying. The Pole himself, provided the interrogation were competently handled, would confess.

"Ah, yes! Hauptman! Let me see."

Lermev handed over the typewritten report that had been sent in by the senior K.G.B. officer on the hydro-electric project. Kitimov read it through with nervous care.

Every Monday Kitimov had meetings with all Heads of Directorates to discuss the more important reports that had been sent in during the week from the various areas. There were several Directorates in the K.G.B. to cover intelligence activity; one for Western Europe, one for Africa, one for South East Asia, one for countries in the Communist bloc, one for the United States alone and one for the internal security in the U.S.S.R. The Directorate of Home Security, of which Lermev was chief, was the largest, most active and most powerful. The K.G.B. had men in every Government ministry, in industry, in Intourist, in foreign embassies, even in the Army. Kitimov spent more time each Monday with Lermev than with any other Head of a Directorate.

"We're not getting anywhere with Hauptman," Kitimov said impatiently, when he had finished reading the report.

"Possibly the charges against him are false, Comrade Colonel."

"You know as well as I do, Alexis, that the Kazan project is six weeks behind schedule. It is obvious that there are subversive forces at work among the staff, and who else could be responsible but this Pole? We already have evidence of his moral degeneracy."

They worked their way through the reports. Kitimov's room, like most other offices in the K.G.B. headquarters, was gloomy and sparsely furnished. A portrait of Kosygin stared down severely from the wall facing the desk. A new regulation had recently been promulgated on the size of official portraits in Government departments, which stipulated that the frames must be several centimetres smaller in both height and width. As a result there was a band of relatively clean paint right round the portrait, showing the area which the previous one had covered.

"What new information have we about this Englishman, Hurford?" Kitimov was asking.

"There is a complete report on his army record." Lermev handed the report across. "You will see that he was parachuted into Yugoslavia to work with the partisans, was captured by the Germans and sentenced to be shot. He managed to escape and after the war was transferred to British Military Intelligence. He spent some time in Trieste, interrogating refugees from Yugoslavia."

"It seems unlikely that even the British would have been so naive as to select a former intelligence officer for an assignment here in Russia, but with the British one never knows. When did he leave the Army?"

"Seven years ago. He resigned his commission and when he was appointed lecturer to the British Institute, he had just been dismissed from a teaching post at a school in the South of France."

Kitimov stared at the report which Lermev had handed him, as though there might be more concealed in it than the typewritten words revealed. Lermev was thinking that Kitimov would be hard to unseat. They were both colonels and had been in the same class at the Frunze Military Academy. In fact Lermev had passed out higher, but Kitimov had been lucky enough to marry the daughter of old Marshal Sherpin.

"I am uneasy about this man, Hurford," Lermev remarked. "It seems to me that there are one or two aspects about his appointment which need to be explained."

"You are quite right, Alexis. We should find out more about the circumstances. Then I shall have to decide whether the facts should be presented to General Godotsky."

Godotsky was head of the K.G.B. and as such a man of the highest importance. Only cases of political significance which might affect relations with foreign powers were taken to him for decision.

"This investigation should be given a higher priority rating," Kitimov said and scribbled instructions on the report. "Instruct your deputy to take charge of the matter personally and arrange for an immediate message to London."

11

HURFORD switched off the light in his bedroom and opened the window. From a drawer in the dressing table he took a pair of binoculars and hung them round his neck. The luminous hands of his watch, which he had just checked for accuracy, showed it was three minutes to ten. The message, if there was to be one, would come at ten precisely.

He stood by the window, looking through the binoculars, and waited. The building which he had to watch was just visible across the roofs of intervening houses, provided that he remained standing. The signal, if it came, would be flashed with an infra-red torch invisible to the naked eye, but his binoculars had a special phosphorous element which turned infra-red into visible rays. His instructions were to watch every Tuesday night at ten o'clock and he had done so conscientiously for two months, but so far there had been no message. If by five-past-ten he had seen nothing, he could abandon his vigil.

Suddenly he saw a light. The unexpectedness of it caused him an instant of confusion and he began trying to read the morse, forgetting that there would be a call sign, repeated three times at intervals of five seconds. One long flash, followed by two short. By the time he had remembered the procedure, the message had begun.

'Seventeen', the light flashed, followed by 'five'. That was all; no repeat. The whole signal was completed in scarcely more than a minute. This was the way to ensure maximum security, they had told him in London.

Hurford shut the window, switched on the light, put away the binoculars and went into the living room of the apartment. The code word 'seventeen' told him that he must go the next day at one o'clock to a restaurant to collect a delivery of information. In the Intourist guide book to Moscow he checked the list of restaurants and saw that number five was the Peking Hotel. There was nothing more to it; a simple routine that made no demands on his initiative nor his intelligence.

Next day he went to the Peking carrying the blue lightweight raincoat and the old Zeiss camera which had been issued to him in London. A waitress showed him to a table half-way down the long room and before sitting down he hung the coat on a peg a few yards away and behind him.

The menu at the Peking was the same as that in all the other large tourist restaurants in Moscow, very long and badly printed. Hurford knew that not more than one-twentieth of the dishes listed would be available. He was pleasantly surprised to find that it also contained three or four Chinese dishes. After even a few weeks he had grown tired of the monotonous, indigestible Russian cooking.

The dish that he chose when it came bore little resemblance to the Chinese food he had eaten in other parts of the world, but he enjoyed it for its novelty. The tiny carafe of vodka which he drank first both sharpened his appetite and dulled his palate.

Afterwards, when he collected his raincoat, he realised as soon as he lifted it from the peg that something had been put into one of the pockets. They had been empty before and even the slight extra weight was immediately noticeable. Though he did not realise the fact, it was not the raincoat he had left hanging there, but another identical one which had been switched with his while he ate. He did not look to see what was in the pocket, but carried the coat away over his arm.

Not till he hung it up on the coat-stand in his office at the Institute, did he examine the consignment that had been planted on him. The envelope he pulled out of the pocket contained a dozen snapshots with an equal number of negatives. The photographs were all views of Moscow: Red Square, the Mausoleum, Svetana's huge statue outside the Exhibition of Economic Achievement, Sokolniki Park of Rest and Culture. They were all the usual tourist snaps and not very expertly taken at that, with badly judged exposures. He held the negatives up against the light from the window. Eight of them matched prints in the envelope. The remaining four were of documents in Russian which appeared to be typewritten reports. Hurford was curious enough to get a magnifying glass, switch on his desk lamp and read a few lines from each. Then he put them back in their envelope and placed it in his breast-pocket.

That evening there was to be a reception at the American Embassy. Hurford had been invited along with members of the British Embassy staff, among them Miss Daphne Dulcet, the queen bee of the secretarial staff. There would be no difficulty in chatting to her about Moscow, showing her the photographs he had taken, lending them to her to show to her colleagues. She would return them in a few days, but without the four negatives which by then would be in London.

12

"EST-CE que tu aimes cette boîte?"

"C'est absolument fab!"

"Tu veux danser?"

"Pas maintenant."

As usual at midnight Don Camilo's was beginning to fill up. People were arriving in parties of four or six and all except one or two of the tables round the dance floor were taken. In dim light the dancers, shaking and twisting, against the red décor, were creations of Dante.

Monique felt the young man's knee rubbing gently against her own beneath the table. She did not mind. In a few moments, no doubt, he would disengage one of his hands which were clasping hers and then she might feel those caressing fingers on her thigh below the mini-skirt. She felt pleasantly expectant, wondering whether the sensation would be as agreeable as more experienced girls at school had suggested.

This was only their second outing together. She had met Roger in another discotheque a week after school had finished and she had come to Paris. He had told her that he was a Scotsman working in France for a whisky firm. That would explain why he had his own bottle of Johnny Walker which they kept for him at Don Camilo's and which he proffered so liberally. At 18 francs a drink or 170 a bottle, most of the young men she knew were prepared to stretch out one glass for a whole evening.

"Have you always lived in Paris?"

"No. My home is in the Midi. I'm just staying in Paris with my uncle and aunt."

"But you have a job here?"

"No. Perhaps later. You see, I only left school a few months ago." She made it months instead of days, afraid that otherwise he might consider her too young. It was only the really old men who preferred young girls and Roger could not be more than twenty-eight.

The music changed from beat to ballad; something slow and sad by Françoise Hardy, as the disc jockey sensed it was the occasion for a more sensuous mood. From his booth he could watch the customers arriving. There had been not so many teen-agers tonight, but a good sprinkling of middle-aged men, accompanied by expensive girls.

"My favourite song!" Monique exclaimed. "Oh, can we dance now?"

They danced for a time, drank more Scotch and danced again. At two-thirty he drove her in his bright red Austin Healey to her uncle's apartment near Etoile.

On the way he asked conversationally: "Where did you go to school?" His French was fluent but bore traces of a guttural accent which she supposed must be Scottish.

"In Nice."

"Really? A friend of my father works in a girl's school at Nice. Still, I suppose it could not be the same school. His name is Michael Hurford."

"Hurford! It isn't possible!"

"Yes. My father served with him in the Army during the war."

Monique laughed unkindly. "It must be the same man, then. He used to teach me English."

"Why do you laugh?"

"But don't you see? It's so funny! He had to leave the school because of me."

"You're joking!"

"It's true! My father complained that Mister Hurford was corrupting me."

"Good God!" Roger looked shocked. "Are you certain it's the same man? The Hurford whom my father knows is a very formal, correct man, an army officer. I don't think he would . . ."

"Roger, chéri, you don't understand! This man didn't do anything to me.

76

As if I would have allowed him to! Why, he's quite old and not very sympathetic." "Then why did your father complain against him?"

"My father would never have done it on his own account. He simply did what my uncle told him to, as he always does."

They had reached the street where she lived and he stopped the car, prudently, a hundred metres away from her uncle's apartment. The houses on each side were impressively elegant. To buy an apartment of any size in one of them would cost at least half a million francs, probably three-quarters of a million. He felt no envy, because his job enabled him, from time to time, to live the life of the rich, without any of its obligations.

"My father is nothing!" Monique exclaimed scornfully. "He works for the Syndicat d' Initiative in Nice and even that job my uncle got him. Now my uncle, he's different. He's rich."

"But you're saying that he wanted to

get my father's friend dismissed from his post at your school. Why on earth would your uncle want that?"

Monique shrugged her bony shoulders. "I expect it has something to with politics."

"Is your uncle a politician then?"

"Yes, he has an important job in the Government." She moved a little nearer to him. "But do we have to talk about him all the time, Roger?"

"We don't need to talk at all."

They kissed for ten minutes; he expertly, she with growing enthusiasm. He felt he could afford to give her that much attention at least. Her breasts, between his fingers, were undeveloped and soft. Oysters, he thought, with amused detachment.

After dropping her outside her uncle's apartment, he drove back by the Champs-Elysées. The girls were out in their smart little cars, hoping to pick up the last Americans as they lurched back to their hotels, frustrated after an evening at the Sexy. He was tempted to stop one of them. Monique, in spite of her immaturity, had stirred the beginnings of lust in him. But duty must come first.

Having parked the Austin Healey at an all-night garage, he walked down the street to where another, much larger, black car stood stationed. He climbed into the driving seat, picked up a chauffeur's cap which lay on the seat alongside and put it on. Then he drove away, heading in the direction of the Russian Embassy.

13

COLONEL FENTON was often taken for an Old Etonian. His shirts were made by New and Lingwood, his suits by Pope and Bradley, his bowler by Locks. Every second Tuesday he had an appointment at Trumpers and came away smelling like any Guards' officer. He was absent from the office during Royal Ascot, bought presents for his family from Dunhills and for his mistress from Aspreys. He never said 'cheers' or sprinkled salt on his vegetables.

To be mistaken for an Old Etonian was good cover. No one could possibly have supposed that a man like Fenton could be engaged in ungentlemanly business. But he had been playing the part so long that he had grown attached to it. Sometimes he even wished he had been to Eton. In truth he had been one of the outstanding intellects at Manchester Grammar and Keble and was disciplined, insensitive and ruthless.

Savage said to him: "The Bureau has picked up something which should interest you."

The Bureau was the name given to the department which carried out desk research for Intelligence. It scrutinised all newspapers and magazines published in the Communist bloc, monitored radio programmes, sifted every item of possible value.

Fenton took the clipping which Savage was holding. It reported that a top-level delegation from the Soviet was to visit Istanbul in six weeks' time. The names of the members of the delegation, all high-ranking Russian officers and civilians, were given.

"You're thinking of the Hurford project?"

"Yes."

"Six weeks doesn't give us much time to capitalise."

"Agreed. But can we afford to miss the chance? It's a fantastic stroke of luck!"

Savage did not have to explain the scheme he was suggesting. Fenton, he knew, had an uncanny ability to see the potential of every situation and to know what kind of plan any of his subordinates would devise to exploit it.

"It would be a damning piece of evidence."

The humour of the idea appealed to Savage's sense of irony. "We can organise an escape route; passport, air tickets, the lot."

"Do we know a friendly bank in Istanbul? One we can trust to be indiscreet."

"No problem."

"Good. And do something with B.E.A. They've always been one of our best loudspeakers in that part of the world."

"In most places if it comes to that. As far as I can see the only thing you need to get a job in an airline is verbal diarrhoea."

They giggled together. No one ever managed to discuss business with Fenton and get away without sharing a joke. He believed it was good for staff relations that he should be known as a man with a sense of fun. In reality the nearest he had ever been to humour was when he shook the hand of Bob Hope at a Forces' concert.

"I'll put a scheme in train immediately," Savage promised.

"How's your pal Hurford making out by the way?"

"Splendidly. He's a first class operator, whatever other limitations he may have. Follows instructions precisely. His stuff has been coming in regularly."

"What about this end?"

"Special Branch has everything it needs now. They'll act as soon as we give the word."

"We mustn't be premature, but I hope to God nothing leaks. We don't want any M.P.s growing nosy.

Intelligence is the pot of gold at the end of the rainbow for an M.P. today. There's no easier way to make a name for yourself than to stir up a big security scandal."

14

A BLACK Hillman pulled up on the unmade road outside a solitary house. A man in a fawn raincoat and brown trilby got out. General Kyle watched him as he came through the gate and up the neglected path. On rainy days there was nothing else to do except stare out of the window across the hills and the heather. The general had already written his memoirs.

He heard Jeanie open the door to the stranger. Some damned salesman, no doubt, hoping to unload a pair of guns or oil-fired central heating or artificial manure. Jeanie, the innocent, would always let them in.

The door to the drawing room opened. "Mr. Partridge, sir. He's from London." Jeanie's voice betrayed her feelings towards the visitor, swaying between distrust for soft spoken strangers and admiration for anyone who made the inconceivable voyage from London to Perthshire.

"General Kyle?"

"Yes. What can I do for you?"

"I'm sorry to disturb you, sir."

The man was erect and respectful, almost certainly a former soldier. The general sighed inwardly. How could one turn away any man down on his luck?

But Partridge pulled an identification card from his pocket and held it out. "Special Branch, sir."

"Oh, Lord, you haven't come about my blasted book again, have you?" The general's memoirs had included two or three indiscreet references to wartime incidents. They had discredited a well-known politician, brought the general twenty thousand in serial rights and aroused the curiosity of the Special Branch.

"Your memoirs? No, sir."

"Ah, read them, did you?"

"Of course. I enjoyed them immensely, sir. So did everyone else who saw action in the desert."

General Kyle was pleased. "What were you? Artillery?"

"No, sir. Armoured Corps."

"Ah, well. Care for a drink?"

Partridge agreed, with the proper show of gratitude for this gesture of acceptance. The general went to the sideboard and poured out two half tumblers of Blair Athol Malt whisky, which he topped up with peaty water.

"How can I help you then, Partridge?"

"It's an enquiry about an officer who was once in your regiment."

"He's not in trouble, I hope."

"Nothing like that at all. As a matter of fact, this chap has applied for a job in which there is a considerable security factor."

"And you're screening him?"

"Exactly."

"Who is this fellow?"

"His name is Hurford, sir. Michael Hurford. He served under you during the war before he was seconded to Intelligence. According to records he . . . "

"I remember Hurford all right. You don't have to prompt my memory. I always used to pride myself that I knew every officer in the regiment, even at the time when they were changing every few weeks. Hurford was with me in Africa. First-class officer."

"His military record is beyond reproach."

"Then what is it you have come five hundred miles to see me about?"

Partridge did not appear exactly uncomfortable but he gave a decent show of reluctance in framing his next remark. "As you know, sir, Hurford resigned his commission."

"Well, what of it? Hundreds of officers did after the war."

"There's a rumour that he resigned as the direct result of an incident in the regiment."

"Rumour? And that's all you're worried about? Hang it all, Partridge, you must know that there are always rumours when a man resigns from the Army. When I was at Wellington we had a young games master who had just resigned his commission and people started to hint that he had been forced to get out after a scandal over mess funds. Years later I found out there was no truth in the story at all. The fellow had got married young and just couldn't afford army life."

"This is a bit more than a rumour." Partridge was stubborn, though still respectful. "We know part of the truth."

"Well, don't go thinking that I'll tell you the rest." It was difficult to know how much of the general's indignation was genuine, how much bluster. "I never was a pedlar of gossip and I've never blackened a man's character."

"Hurford knows that we are approaching you. He gave us your name as a reference."

"Bloody fine reference it would be

if I start scandalising about his private life."

Partridge stared at the general for a moment thoughtfully. Then he swallowed the rest of his whisky and put the glass down. "I fully appreciate your feelings, General, and between ourselves I was sure you would see it that way."

"I'm glad to hear it."

"Of course, it won't help poor Hurford," Partridge added, almost sorrowfully as he moved towards the door. "So long as there is any shadow of doubt, I'm afraid my superiors will never give him a clearance. It's damned inhuman, but in a way understandable I suppose."

"But there was nothing in this incident that would affect his security rating."

"Even so."

The general hesitated. It was difficult to go counter to the habits that years of esprit de corps had conditioned, but if it would help one of his officers he could discipline himself to sacrifice.

"It was that man Norris who was to blame. Never cared much for Norris. Good soldier but couldn't keep his hands off the girls. And the women couldn't keep away from him. There would have been no harm in that till he started on his fellow officers' wives. Before the war a man would have been kicked out of the service for that."

"Are you saying that he had an affair with Hurford's wife?"

"Exactly." The general's eyes wrinkled in distaste. They were blue eyes, very faded; eyes that had looked over vast spaces, death, boredom, deserts and other men's debaucheries. "Norris picked up with Margery first when Hurford was in Yugoslavia. Nasty, you'll agree, but typical. I had him posted. Then after the war when Hurford was seconded to Intelligence, they met up again and it all started once more."

"But how did this lead to Hurford leaving the Army? He didn't just resign his commission to get away?"

"Of course not! He could have gone back to the regiment. I'd have taken him back like a shot."

"Then?"

The general steeled himself to unpleasantness. "Hurford lost control. Can't blame the man for that, but he went for Norris with a knife. Cut him up quite badly. It would have been all right if he had given him a good thrashing. But a knife!"

Partridge, who knew a thing or two about knives, restrained a smile. "I suppose it was natural in a way. After all they must have taught him to use one in Yugoslavia. There was a court martial, I presume?"

"No. Norris had the decency at least not to make a complaint. Put about a story that he had been beaten up by thugs on his way back to camp. Very properly the incident was hushed up. But Hurford's C.O. hadn't much choice except to take his resignation. Billie Brabington-Smith. He and I were at Sandhurst together."

Walking away down the garden path after a final conciliatory whisky, Partridge decided that the ways of Englishmen were not so very strange after all. The story of Hurford's disgrace reminded him of a remarkably similar incident that had involved one of his friends when they were both at the Moscow Military Academy.

15

THE Director General of the K.G.B., Marshal Godotsky, was a man with a reputation that many people admired and still more envied. To a fine military record, including an outstanding victory in the Finnish campaign, he had added administrative achievements of an impressive order.

He had been called in to reorganise the K.G.B. at a time when both efficiency and morale were low after a succession of setbacks abroad, culminating in the arrest of Lonsdale by British Intelligence. Another major factor in his success was the fact that he had no political ambitions.

"Comrade Marshal," Kitimov said. "We have a case in the Directorate of Internal Security which I believe must be brought to your attention."

Godotsky's expression remained impassive except that amusement wrinkled the skin around his eyes briefly. "The Englishman Hurford?"

"You know about him?"

"I try to keep myself up to date, Citizen Colonel."

Kitimov looked sharply at Lermev who sat beside him facing the Marshal across his desk. Was it possible that he had been going over his head?

"We have irrefutable evidence that Hurford was sent in to Russia by British Intelligence."

Godotsky waited, listening. He was an experienced listener. Kitimov told him about the investigations which the K.G.B. had initiated in Paris.

"What is your opinion then?" Godotsky asked. "That the dismissal from the school was just part of his cover?"

"There is no other explanation."

"Have you his dossier there?"

Lermev handed the file across to him and Godotsky glanced through it quickly. The other two men waited. Through the window Lermev saw three jet fighters pass. Their vapour trails were like pipe-cleaners being dragged towards infinity. Kitimov was speculating whether his father-in-law was still as influential as he imagined.

"The evidence is strong but not conclusive," Godotsky said at last. "What interests me more is why this man Hurford was selected for whatever assignment British Intelligence had in mind."

"He speaks Russian fluently," Lermev remarked. "And of course he has past experience of this type of work."

"Most people would say that was a liability rather than an advantage. It weakens his cover."

"I have been thinking about that, Comrade Marshal. It could be a double bluff."

"His record in the British Army was exceptional," Lermev added.

"Agreed. But subsequently he disgraced himself. Consider this. Here is a man who emotionally cannot be entirely stable. He attacked another officer with a knife. Knowing that would you have chosen him for operations overseas?"

"Never, Comrade Marshal."

Kitimov suggested, "We could arrange for him to be recalled. The British Institute here is a special concession granted under diplomatic convention."

"Then we would never discover why he was sent to Moscow. No, I believe it would be better strategy to let things run for a while."

"But he has been here for two months already!"

"Even so. We have to remember also that it is the policy of the Council of Ministers to sustain the present good relations with Britain."

"Then we must place him under twenty-four-hour surveillance," Kitimov said firmly.

"Can Comrade Lermev spare the men?" Godotsky asked.

"Only with extreme difficulty, Comrade Marshal. We are desperately understaffed."

"In that case put on an intensive random surveillance."

Random surveillance was a system by which a suspect was watched and followed for periods of six or eight hours at random intervals, usually not less than once every eight days. All members of foreign diplomatic missions were kept under random surveillance. Under intensive random surveillance the frequency of these periods was increased, all the suspect's telephone calls were tapped and selected examples of his mail opened.

"Are you sure this is wise?" Kitimov persisted.

"Under present circumstances it will be enough. Report to me personally if there are any further developments."

16

HURFORD waited for ten minutes at the withdrawals desk of the Lenin Library. Like everywhere else in Moscow one had to queue, to wait one's turn. It was the same in the restaurants, the shops and the banks. He had begun to suspect that it must be official policy to keep them understaffed and thus to reduce people, through long hours of waiting, to docile apathy.

Eventually a plump woman with straight hair fetched him the two books for which he had asked. As a foreigner he had to have a special authority to borrow books from the library.

His instructions had reached him that morning by shortwave radio. The set which had been provided for him by Equipment Section could be tuned very easily to a certain wave-length on which each morning from eight to nine there was a programme of pop music. Hurford listened to it without fail every Saturday, waiting for coded instructions which might or might not come in an innocuous sentence in the disc jockey's puerile chatter.

As well as to visit the library, he had been instructed to collect an envelope from a dead drop that evening and deposit it in another cache the next day. With two commissions on the same day his operation in Moscow was being raised to a pace which was more to his liking. To counter the growing loneliness that was beginning to envelop him, he needed action. The nature of a spy's work in peacetime, he realised now, precluded almost any form of human relationship except the most superficial. In any case the only people in Moscow with whom he might have cultivated friendship were the British Embassy staff. Too close a contact with Russians would have been suspect. Nationals of other countries, tourists, businessmen, actors, were only in Russia on short visits. The Embassy people, for their part, had put out fenders, like sailors warding off a plague-ridden ship that threatened to come alongside. Whatever Savage might believe in London, they all knew or suspected Hurford's real occupation.

He took the two books from the librarian. They were both on the subject of cybernetics; one being written in Russian and the other in German. Hurford understood now why he had been made to read a monograph on cybernetics as part of his Russian course at the Institute's headquarters in London.

On the Metro, travelling back to his apartment he took the standard security precautions, boarding trains at the last possible moment, changing stations and doubling back on his tracks. At no time was there the slightest evidence that he was being followed.

In his apartment he opened the two

books, fetched a magnifying glass and a razor blade and set to work. The microdots were where he had been told they would be, neatly fixed to cover fullstops, in one book at the seventh line of page forty-nine and in the other at the seventeenth line of page seventy-seven. Hurford prised them away carefully with the razor blade, six microdots in all. Afterwards on a portable typewriter he composed a letter to Peter Noddick, an old university friend. With a special adhesive issued to him back in London, he transferred the microdots to suitable places on the letter, which he then placed in an envelope addressed to Noddick's home in Bristol. Noddick had probably moved away or gone abroad. He might even be dead. It was of no consequence because the letter was not meant to reach him. When the diplomatic bag reached London the envelope would be quietly removed.

By the time his work was finished, it was three-thirty. He was due to lecture at the Institute on the English Romantic Poets at five o'clock. There was ample time to call at the British Consulate and leave his letter there. Later that evening on his way back from the Institute he would be able to pick up the packet from the dead drop. These things were better done in darkness.

Putting on his raincoat, he slipped the letter into his pocket and left the apartment. The sky had clouded over and it was beginning to rain, a light drizzle coming from the West, that carried the smell of damp earth. Two men in blue mackintoshes and brown hats were standing on the other side of Sadovaya Samotechnaya. A large black car was parked fifty yards down the street from them. Hurford noticed the men and the car, but only because he had been trained to observe and not with any sense of imminent danger. When he crossed the street and headed for the bus stop, the men moved in to intercept him.

"You are Gospodin Hurford?"

"That's right."

"We would like you to come with us."

"Who are you?"

Simultaneously they pulled out their identification cards and thrust them in front of him.

"K.G.B."

"What do you want?"

"Our instructions are to take you to headquarters for questioning."

Part Two

Exposure

17

THE K.G.B. men escorted Hurford to their car in which a uniformed driver was waiting. He sat in the back between them and the car moved off towards the centre of Moscow. After a short distance the driver turned to the left and he knew then that they were not taking him to K.G.B. headquarters.

Ten minutes later they pulled up outside the Lubianka prison. The gates were opened by a uniformed guard and the car swung into a yard before the prison building. Analysing his emotions, Hurford found not fear, but a sharpening of the senses. It was as though at last he found himself facing the danger that was his real mission in Russia. The idea was, he knew, illogical and without foundation. Savage would have laughed mockingly. He was not a force in the game of espionage, not even an agent. He was a fly, a scavenger of other people's information and like any other fly he had flown at last headlong into the web.

He was taken along a corridor to a bare room. There a young woman, not much past twenty-five and strongly built, was waiting and the guards left him with her. Hurford could not even remember their faces; two anonymous men who had done their anonymous duty.

"Undress," the woman ordered him brusquely.

He took off his raincoat and the jacket of his suit and then stopped, uncertain what she expected.

"Undress, I said!"

Reluctantly he obeyed, undoing his tie and discarding first shirt, then trousers. He was aware, self-consciously, that his pale blue cotton vest had a number of tiny holes in the region of the neck, where moths had been at work the previous summer. "Undress!"

the woman shouted.

As he took off his shoes, socks and underclothes, Hurford decided that he had never before undressed to a woman's orders. It caused him no embarrassment, only irritation. The choice of a woman for this chore was typical of Russian methods, intended to humiliate.

The woman made him lift his arms and stand with his legs astride. Then she searched him minutely; hair, ears, nostrils and every other cavity where anything might possibly have been concealed. The search over, she smiled as though she were pleased that he had passed this test, slapped him unexpectedly in the small of the back and went outside.

Almost immediately a guard in uniform came in, carrying a knife with a broad six-inch blade. Instinctively Hurford flinched. The man took no notice of him, however, but began picking up his clothes. After carefully feeling the shirt, underclothes, tie, socks, and finding nothing, he set to work on Hurford's suit, ripping open the lining and slashing the pockets. Next he slit the sole of each shoe apart and tried, with the point of the knife, to prise off the heels.

"And what am I supposed to wear when you've finished?" Hurford asked the man sarcastically.

Without replying the guard left the room and came back with a jacket and trousers. He said: "You will wear these while the lining of your suit is being repaired."

Hurford put on his own shirt and underclothes, followed by the prison suit. It was drab brown in colour and made of a coarse woollen material. As a fit the length was not unreasonable but in the waist the trousers were at least six inches too large. He asked the Russian guard if he might have a belt or a pair of braces.

"In no circumstances are prisoners permitted to have either. Nor shoe-laces."

He picked up Hurford's shoes and, when he had extracted the laces, threw them across to him. "Put those on and come with me."

They left the reception room and walked down a long corridor. Hurford could only shuffle along by the side of the guard, holding his trousers up and scarcely able to lift his feet for fear of losing his shoes. At the end of the corridor they came to a large metal door with a bell push in the wall beside it. The guard rang the bell and another man in uniform opened the door to them. As it shut behind him with an echoing finality, Hurford had to fight against a feeling of hopelessness. It was too easy to believe that he would never pass back through the door to liberty.

The guard led him along a second corridor, walking by his side. The walls were painted a dark grey up to a height of about four feet and a discoloured cream above. For some reason the corridor reminded Hurford of a passage in the old-fashioned offices of a steelworks in Rotherham which he had visited as a boy. The walls had the same depressing air of permanence, reminding one that they would still be there long after men were dead and forgotten.

As they walked along, the guard made a clicking noise with his tongue not unlike a coachman encouraging a team of horses At one point, approaching a bend in the passage, they heard a similar noise coming towards them. Rounding the bend, they found another guard standing by a prisoner who stood turned away from them, face and hands flat to the wall. It was a rule in the Lubianka that prisoners should never have an opportunity to recognise or communicate with each other and the warning signals of the guards were directed to this end.

They passed through another door, along a third passage and into a large hall, on both sides of which the cells were situated. A staircase led to an upper floor where there were more cell doors. On both floors guards were patrolling up and down outside the cells.

A duty officer at a desk recorded Hurford's arrival in a book and gave the guard who had escorted him a receipt. The cell which had been prepared for his arrival was number 82. As they showed him in, Hurford remembered that the numbers 8 and 2 he had always supposed to be lucky for him.

The cell was painted dark green and its furniture consisted of an iron bed, a table and a bucket. A black enamel mug stood empty on the table and for bedclothes there was a single blanket on a mattress. Although the room was hot and airless, it smelt overpoweringly of damp and another, indefinable smell which might have been human sweat. In the door there was a small aperture which could be opened from the outside so that the guards could keep watch on the prisoners. Above the door a powerful electric light bulb, encased in a wire cage, shone brightly. The only daylight came through a small barred window set in the wall opposite the door well above eye level.

Without speaking the guard went out and shut the door, leaving Hurford alone. Although there were cells on each side of and above his own and although the guards walked up and down the hall outside incessantly, the silence was frightening.

18

"WE have until tomorrow morning at least."

"That will be long enough."

"But the British Embassy will know of his arrest by then."

"Don't worry about the Embassy," Kitimov replied. "They can do nothing."

"Except inform the Western press. Then the story will be out."

Although it was after midnight, Kitimov was still in his office at K.G.B. headquarters with his subordinate, Lermev. Outside the streets were deserted except for an occasional drunk whom the police had not yet picked up and charged with his social offence. The restaurants were closed, the theatre performances long since over. Good Soviet citizens should be either in bed or reading a last chapter from their textbooks.

"I still think it might have been wiser to consult Godotsky," Lermev persisted.

"There was not the possibility of doing that. As usual he has left Moscow for his house in the country till Monday. There he has no telephone."

"We could have postponed arresting the man and kept him under constant surveillance."

"And allow even more information to pass back to London? Who knows the danger that may have already been caused to our national security by Hurford?"

"But we have no evidence to show that he was likely to send back anything before Monday."

"He was on his way to the British Embassy with messages when we picked him up."

"How do you know?" Lermev asked.

"My source is absolutely reliable."

They continued arguing, Kitimov to justify his decision not to his subordinate, but to himself; Lermev for the record, because he secretly hoped that at last the upstart had overreached himself.

At twenty-five minutes past one, there was a knock on the door. Sherdin, deputy head of the K.G.B. investigation laboratories, came in. He was a technologist, inconspicuous except for his monstrous bald skull, and married to a cousin of Kitimov.

"Well?" Kitimov demanded impatiently.

"We have examined all his clothes and everything that was found in his pockets."

"And you found nothing?"

Sherdin smiled, savouring a rare moment of satisfaction. "On the contrary, Citizen Colonel, here you have all the evidence you need."

Carefully, like a Bond Street jeweller unwrapping a priceless diamond, he placed before Kitimov the letter which Hurford had been carrying in his raincoat pocket when the K.G.B. had picked him up.

"There. See the microdots?"

Kitimov ran his finger over the surface of the paper and laughed with nervous pleasure. "Excellent Mikhail!! I knew we'd find the evidence."

"But do we know what the microdots contain?" Lermev tried to conceal his disappointment. It was just like Kitimov to be saved by a piece of undeserved luck.

Sherdin replied: "I took them off and made enlargements of each. Then I pasted them back in their original positions. The regulations stipulate that evidence must be left in its original form."

He handed Kitimov six whole-plate photographic enlargements. One of them listed payments made to K.G.B. agents by the Soviet Embassy in Lisbon. Two reproduced a report from an agent in America on an experimental missile launching system recently installed in a Polaris submarine. The remainder comprised a complete list of the last class to graduate from the K.G.B. training school in Leningrad.

"You may go, Citizen Sherdin," he said stiffly. "I will keep all this material here."

After Sherdin had left he pushed the photographs over to Lermev grimly. "This is far worse than I imagined."

"But Citizen Colonel, this is all material from K.G.B. headquarters."

"Exactly! Hurford's contact must be a member of our staff."

For a long time neither man spoke. For the first time that evening their thoughts were attuned, their feelings identical. If it were proved that someone in the K.G.B. had been working for the West, some of the suspicion and disgrace would rub off on to all of them. There would be a top-level inquiry, suspensions, perhaps charges of negligence.

"We must keep this to ourselves for as long as we possibly can," Kitimov said at last.

"But Marshal Godotsky will have to be told."

"Of course. He is in it like the rest of us."

19

FOR six days Hurford remained alone in his cell. Twice a day, for ten minutes in the morning and again in the evening, he was allowed to go, escorted by a guard, to the ablutions. Three times a day food was brought to him. Otherwise there was only a vigilant eye, glancing every twenty minutes or so through the Judas window of the cell door, to remind him that anyone outside was aware of his existence. In all six days not a single word was said to him. The guards, when they wished to, communicated with signs and if he spoke to them, they did not reply.

His immediate reaction to his arrest had been not fear but irritation. He had not lasted long in the spy game. To have staked so much and achieved so little seemed pathetically wasteful.

London would no doubt be wringing their hands, but at least their precious agent, the first-class source of which Savage had spoken, remained undetected. They would only need to find a new courier.

The source was what the K.G.B. would want to identify. It would not take them long to realise, if they did not already know, that he was only a pawn, a messenger. Then they would put all the pressure they could on him, but his position was impregnable. No inquisition in the world could extract from him a name that he did not know. Now he understood the reason behind Savage's elaborate precautions and the complex system of working they had devised for him.

Secure in this knowledge, he slept well the first night, in spite of the fact that the light over the door of the cell was left switched on. When he tried to turn his head away, a guard came in almost at once, shook him and indicated that he must not try to sleep facing the wall.

In the morning he still felt reasonably cheerful. The breakfast brought to him consisted of a thick slice of coarse bread, lightly spread with margarine, and a sweet, watery liquid which was poured into his mug and which he supposed was tea. He finished the food, not because it was in any sense appetising, but he felt that he would need every part of its meagre nourishment to keep up his strength.

Following the same line of reasoning, after breakfast he took exercise, walking up and down his cell. Six paces to the wall and six back to the door; he strode them counting methodically until he estimated he had covered two thousand metres. In the afternoon, following a meal of soup and tea, he walked a similar distance.

From what he had read in the past, he suspected that in Russia the interrogation of suspected agents was protracted, stretching into weeks and even months. The first thing to do was to plan his strategy. Sitting down on

122

the bed, he tried to analyse scientifically the strengths and weaknesses of his position. So far as he knew, the Russians had no proof against him. No doubt he had been kept under surveillance by the K.G.B. for weeks, but any evidence they might have collected would be flimsy and purely circumstantial. Clearly they must have arrested him on suspicion alone.

Unless of course, he told himself, you slipped up somewhere.

A tiny shaft of anxiety pierced his composure. In his mind he carefully went over every operation he had undertaken since his arrival in Moscow. His instructions had been followed without a single deviation, his material delivered always to a contact at the Embassy.

Could the blunder have been made at the end, he wondered. Had one of those effete young men whom the country now saw fit to employ as diplomats, made a hash of things? Perhaps one of them was working for the Russians and had betrayed him.

This idea, superficially unlikely, grew gradually more attractive. It would explain so much. Why else should the Russians have arrested him suddenly and without evidence? He began to examine each of the Embassy officials, measuring their qualifications for the role of Judas.

During the second night, after being wakened by one of the guards for sleeping with his head turned away from the light, he could not fall asleep again. Instead he lay awake for long hours obsessed with an urge to know who had tipped off the K.G.B.

But the riddle stayed with him, needling him into frustrated nervousness, injecting a constant stimulus into his brain every time he sought relaxation in other thoughts. During the day he could find temporary diversion in the routines of eating, exercise and his visits to the ablutions. In the end solitude and silence always drove his brain back into the same labyrinth.

The third night he barely slept at all. When he did, his sleep was floodlit with grotesque dreams. From one of them he woke to find himself lying stretched out with rigid limbs, hands folded above his chest, eyes staring at the dark green ceiling, a plaster saint, immobile on his tomb. He had the frightening feeling that he had surprised himself in the act of death.

The Lubianka, as always, was silent. Through the barred window of the cell came a faint noise which might have been rain. The notion that outside rain might be falling softened the tensions of his mind. Might it not also be raining in the South of France, he wondered; a midnight shower that would settle the summer heat, allowing the sun to shine brightly next morning on a town refreshed. He remembered too that it had been raining when they arrested him.

"My God!" he said suddenly and aloud, sitting up in alarm. "My raincoat!"

He had been wearing the raincoat when the K.G.B. men stopped him and in the pocket was the letter to Peter Noddick, with its incriminating microdots. For an inexplicable reason he had forgotten about the letter at the time of his arrest and ever since. His mind, numbed with shock or confusion, had rejected the letter, like a psychopath rejecting the memory of an act whose consequences had been painful.

Now he could not even remember whether they had taken the coat from him. He had no recollection of removing it when he undressed before the virile female examiner. Surely if they had slashed it open as they had his suit, he would have noticed and become aware of the danger?

The shutter of the Judas window in the cell door was pulled back and a guard stared in at him. Instinctively, already conditioned to obedience, he lay back on the bed.

If the K.G.B. found the microdots in the letter, that would be evidence of his activities. Enough to hang a man, he thought. Or was it the firing squad that they used to eliminate the enemies of the Soviet? He tried to tell himself that they would not scrutinise the letter unless they had already been tipped off about him, but this did nothing to lessen his anxiety. The problem of who might or might not have betrayed him no longer seemed to matter. Toothache had been deadened by the biting pain of a malignant tumour.

Until morning he lay awake worrying about the letter. It seemed inconceivable that they would not have opened it and found the microdots. On the other hand if they had this evidence, why had he not been confronted with it? Why had he not been formally charged with espionage?

By the fourth day he no longer had any appetite for the unvarying diet of prison food. At breakfast he forced himself to swallow half of the thick slab of bread and then, afraid that if he left any uneaten his ration might be reduced, hid the remainder beneath his folded blanket.

On his way with a guard to the ablutions, he passed another prisoner in the corridor. The man's face, pressed against the wall, was hidden from him but something in his build or in the shape of his head seemed familiar. The idea that it might have been somebody he knew nagged at him all day, intruding on his preoccupation with the letter and the microdots.

Late in the afternoon, after discarding a score of possibilities, he decided that the man had been Dixon, the Cultural Attaché at the British Embassy and one of the people who had transmitted his information to London. If they've got him too, he thought, the balloon really has gone up, they've split our whole organisation open.

Then he remembered Dixon would be covered by diplomatic immunity. He must have been mistaken. And yet the shape of that head was distinctive. Could the Russians possibly have flouted convention and pulled a member of the Embassy staff into the Lubianka?

This possibility was a new cause of anxiety and he brooded over it into the night. The net, he was convinced, was beginning to tighten around him. It was not fear of the prospect of punishment and death that worried him, but uncertainty. He had an overwhelming urge to know how badly he had failed, how much of the intricate structure of British Intelligence he had pulled down with him.

"Why in God's name don't they accuse me, question me?" he complained aloud. "I wish to hell something would happen."

20

TWO mornings later he had his wish. A guard led him from the ablutions out of the prison hall, up a staircase and along a corridor to the interrogation rooms. The assistant from the Prosecutor's Department who waited for him in room seven was a young man with a sharp, intelligent face. With his high forehead and cheekbones he was no Slav but had alien blood, probably from the Baltic.

"Well, Hurford," he said affably. "We need not waste any time on preliminaries. As you can see we have all the evidence we need of your guilt."

On the desk in front of him lay Hurford's letter to Noddick and beside it six blown-up photographs of documents in Russian.

"What is all this?" Hurford asked.

"You don't deny that this letter was

in your possession yesterday afternoon? See, it bears your signature."

"I don't deny it. That's a letter to a friend of mine in England. I was taking it to the post when your agents arrested me."

"To the post? The envelope is not stamped. Are you sure you were not on your way to the British Embassy where the letter would have been sent through the diplomatic bag?"

"I was going to buy a stamp." The lie came smoothly, although Hurford had not prepared it. "And even if I were going to send the letter through the Embassy, that's not an offence as far as I know."

"Passing classified information to another power is an offence here, just as in your own country." The Prosecutor's man pushed the photographs towards Hurford. "Concealed in your letter we found six microdots and these are the enlargements. They are all of documents from the confidential files of a Soviet Ministry.

What can you say to that?"

Picking up the photographs Hurford glanced through them. Some of the documents which they had reproduced were official reports addressed to K.G.B. headquarters from their agents. He had no time to see any more than this before the Prosecutor's man took the enlargements back.

"If you found these in my letter, then they must have been planted there by the K.G.B."

"Come, you really can't expect me to believe that!"

"Why not? It wouldn't be the first time that Soviet Intelligence had planted evidence on a man whom they wished to convict."

"My dear Hurford, what possible reason could we have for wishing to victimise you, a lecturer at the British Institute? Do you imagine that you are so important to us?"

"I still maintain that your evidence was planted." Hurford chose his words with care. "And that is what

I'll say at the trial."

"Trial? What makes you believe we are planning to try you?"

Playing with words, hypothetical discussions, could be dangerous, Hurford reasoned. This man was a trained lawyer with a mind schooled to the dialectic art. Like a prisoner of war he must at all costs avoid being drawn into arguments.

"I have nothing to say." The words as he said them sounded theatrical.

"It would be a pity if you were to persist in that attitude. You see we already have enough evidence of your espionage. On the other hand if you were to be co-operative, things would be made a great deal easier for you."

"How much co-operation would you expect?"

"The names of your contacts in Russia and a summary of all the information you have sent back to London."

"I have no contacts, as you describe them, so I can't help you."

The Prosecutor's assistant began collecting together the papers in front of him. "Well, it isn't important but it would be tidier if you were to make a full admission."

"So you could have a full-scale propaganda trial?"

"You appear to be obsessed with the notion that you are going to be given a trial."

"What's the alternative? Presumably you have no intention of releasing me?"

"Indeed not." The Prosecutor's assistant smiled. For the first time since he had been arrested, Hurford felt a sensation of expectancy, of tension.

"Then what?"

"We intend to dispose of this matter with the greatest possible speed and the minimum of trouble. In the Soviet Union, espionage is a military offence. You will appear before a military tribunal of the Supreme Court this afternoon. In view of the evidence which we have against you, I must say that the proceedings are unlikely to be more than a formality."

A guard took Hurford back to his cell. There, sitting on his bed, he began to realise that things were not running his way. What chiefly made him uneasy was the brevity of his examination by the Prosecutor. He had been expecting an intensive cross-questioning with every possible pressure brought on him, but the Prosecutor had made only a token effort to persuade him into a confession. It could be just bluff, but the Prosecutor's assistant had seemed ominously assured, as though a decision had already been taken and all he had to do was to carry it out.

Doubt began to filter into his mind, not about his fate but about his ability to see this thing through. Twenty years before he had found in himself the resilience, the capacity to endure mental as well as physical pressure. Now he suspected that, like an ageing boxer, there were limits to the punishment he could absorb.

After the usual lunch of soup, black bread and tea, he was again taken upstairs, not to the interrogation room this time, but to a small ante-room in another wing. Two soldiers were waiting there and they escorted him, one in front and one following, through a pair of swing doors.

Beyond there was a small courtroom, furnished in a more imposing style, but still austere and lifeless. The lifelessness was accentuated by the fact that it was almost empty. At a desk to the left sat an army officer, a colonel as far as Hurford could tell, and the Prosecutor's assistant. Opposite the entrance was a high raised desk behind which three more officers sat waiting. A clerk in sergeant's uniform was writing at a small table in front of the bench.

His escort led Hurford to a single chair in the middle of the room. When they halted the clerk looked up and called out: "The Military Tribunal of the Supreme Court of the Union of Socialist Soviet Republics is now in session. Colonel Tutin presides."

The proceedings of the court could scarcely have been briefer. First the officer sitting next to the Prosecutor's assistant and presumably his military equivalent, read a statement describing the circumstances of Hurford's arrest and the evidence of espionage that had been found in his possession. This proved clearly, he went on to claim, that the prisoner had been passing classified information to a foreign power. He passed Hurford's letter to Noddick and the enlargements of the microdots to the tribunal, each of whom studied them carefully.

"Has the prisoner anything to say?" the President of the court asked.

"Only that this evidence is false. The microdots must have been fixed to my letter after I had been arrested."

"We cannot accept that defence. The letter was opened and examined in the presence of two witnesses, who have testified that it was not tampered with in any way."

Hurford could think of no comment to make. The colonel asked him: "Are there any questions which the prisoner would like to put to the Prosecuting Officer?"

"Yes. I would like to ask him if this is the only evidence he has to offer, why I was arrested before the authorities could have seen it?"

"That question has no relevance to these proceedings."

The Prosecuting Officer then addressed the tribunal, pointing out that Hurford had clearly been sent to Moscow as a British agent. He had been there for several months and it was reasonable to infer that he had passed other information back to Britain. The documents he had photographed were of a military nature and he himself was an army officer posing as a teacher. In the circumstances his offences were subject to military law and demanded the punishments laid down in the military penal code.

The three members of the tribunal

conferred among themselves. One of the soldiers standing behind Hurford pulled at his sleeve and told him in a whisper to stand. The President stared at him as he gave his judgement.

"We find that the prisoner has contravened Articles 78, 96 and 189 of Soviet Military Law and his punishment must be that prescribed in the regulations. Our orders are that he should be executed without delay. There is no right of appeal against this sentence!"

21

SUNLIGHT falling across his face woke Hurford. Shutting his eyes he rolled over and away from it. Sleep still dragged at him. He felt unbelievably tired, all energy drained away, and at the same time a sensation of insensibility, as though all his nerves and his perception had been heavily insulated. The last thing he could remember was eating the meal which had been brought to him the previous evening. Earlier memories, his appearance before the tribunal, seemed strangely remote and unreal, no more than incidents from a book carelessly read and now half forgotten.

God, he thought suddenly, they have executed me and I am dead.

The stone wall next to his face was comfortingly solid and mortal. Slowly he became aware that it was a different colour to the wall he had stared at for the previous week. And sunlight? There had been no sunlight in his cell before.

Turning over, he sat up to look around him. There was no doubt at all. He was in a different cell. The room was larger, the window big enough and low enough for sunlight to come slanting through and for him to see a square of blue sky. They had moved him in the night and first they must have drugged him. It would have been simple enough to mix a sedative in the food.

As his mind wrestled lazily with the implications of this discovery, from outside the window of the cell came noises that were oddly familiar. Boots on a parade ground, marching feet, distant at first but moving nearer. There were words of command too, in Russian. The marching footsteps stopped for a time and then started again. It could be a morning parade or merely foot drill. So they had moved him not just to another cell but to another prison. There was no parade ground outside the Lubianka.

A short time later two guards came in, one carrying his breakfast and the other a light blue woollen jacket. The food was a much better meal than any he had so far been given. There were two boiled eggs on the tray, white bread and butter and a jug of coffee. The blue jacket was laid on his bed. He noticed that it had a diamond-shaped patch of red material in the centre of the back.

"Take off your coat and put this on," one of the men told him.

"Why?"

The man who had given it to him laughed. "The red patch makes a good target."

Hurford did as they ordered and they waited until he had finished eating. Then they took the tray and his former prison jacket away. A few minutes later the door was opened again and a man was ushered in. He wore the clothes of a priest.

"Good morning. I hope I am not disturbing you."

"Not at all."

"They let me come because I understand you are a Catholic."

"Yes, Father, but I didn't know there were any priests still in Russia."

"I am a priest at the French Embassy in Moscow. We have a French church here, you know."

Hurford said nothing. It was fully five years since he had been alone with a priest and he felt ill-at-ease. The man's presence was a reminder of the vast unshed burden of sin that he carried, adultery, lying, failure to go to Mass, neglect of his religious duties.

"Why have you come, Father?" he asked at last.

The priest looked surprised. "I thought that I might be able to offer you some comfort."

"It is a long time since I made any religious observance."

"Even so, at a time like this many

143

men's thoughts turn to God."

At first Hurford's brain, still heavy with the after-effects of the drug, did not absorb the significance of the priest's words.

"If you wish I can hear your confession or say Mass. It may give you strength."

Strength? For what? Suddenly Hurford remembered the military tribunal and the sentence that had been passed on him. Now he understood why he had been moved to another prison, why he was wearing the blue jacket and why he had been sent a priest.

"Does this mean I'm to be executed?" he asked bluntly.

The priest seemed embarrassed. "But I understood you knew!"

"I didn't know it was to be today."

For several minutes neither man spoke. Hurford had the sensation that he was no longer involved in reality. He was watching from a distance a scene in which characters moved and spoke, but one in which he no longer had any control over words or events.

"Is there anything I can do?" the priest asked again.

"No, Father. I don't feel ready for confession."

"We could talk for a while."

"Thank you, but I'd prefer to be alone."

"Very well, my son."

Alone Hurford looked up at the sunlight framed in the window. It needed all his imagination to convince himself that soon, in an hour perhaps or less, that sun would be extinguished. How, he wondered, would they execute him. A lethal injection seemed the method most in keeping with the Russian's passion for science.

As if to answer his speculation, there came again through the window the sound of marching men. There were a smaller number this time, eight perhaps or twelve, and they appeared to be marching away across the parade ground. He heard a shouted command to halt and then a long silence.

Suddenly more commands, sharp and incisive.

"Load. Take aim. Fire."

A volley of shots rang out, almost but not exactly synchronised.

22

AT half-past-four, when the sun had sunk so far that it could no longer be seen through the window of the cell, two soldiers came in to Hurford. As soon as the bolts were drawn back and he caught sight of the uniforms, fear gripped him like an iron claw.

This is it, he told himself, but his mind could not absorb the enormity of the truth. The guards made him stand up and began to handcuff his wrists behind him.

If he was to pray, this was the time for it. "Hail Mary," he began but the words failed him. He tried to compose his thoughts, to think of repentance, but his imagination was being swallowed by a smothering darkness. In the middle of a void was a tiny, dwindling speck of light that he recognised as himself. One of the soldiers started to blindfold him.

"I don't need that." The voice which spoke could not have been his own and the words were empty. More than anything he needed the comfort of darkness.

"We have our orders."

They led him out of the cell and along what must have been a corridor. Then came a door, a short flight of steps leading upwards and another door which had to be unbolted. Feeling cold air against his face, he knew that they were outside and stiffened himself for the last walk across the parade ground. The firing squad, he supposed, were ready in position.

But they only walked a few paces before he was helped up two steps and made to sit down. The seat was hard and not upholstered. There was a smell of inferior petrol. Near at hand a metal door banged, an engine fired and he felt a jerk forward that could only have been a truck pulling away.

I'm being driven out there, he

thought, they can't trust me to walk, afraid my legs might collapse through funk.

The tumbril rolled on slowly. Every second he expected it to stop and to hear the order to descend. Instead they drove on for seconds that lengthened into minutes, for yards that became miles. From outside came the muffled sound of traffic.

Hope, incredulous, sparked for an instant. Were they taking him back to the Lubianka? He thrust the idea from him.

For what must have been an hour the journey continued. Hurford sat there, blindfolded, suspense and fear slowly ebbing to be replaced by hopelessness. Even if this was not to be the moment of annihilation, it would only be deferred. They had passed sentence on him. There was no escape, nothing to hope for except a prolonging.

At last the truck stopped. He was led out, through a door, down more steps and along a series of corridors.

When they removed the blindfold, he was in yet another cell, similar in shape to the one which he had occupied in the Lubianka, but slightly larger. There was also more furniture; beside the bed a table and two chairs, a small strip of carpet on the ground. He could not help thinking that the cell looked more permanent, more suited to a longer stay.

He was left alone in the cell while day turned into darkness. A guard brought him food; soup, bread and tea again. Then I am back at the Lubianka, he decided, on this slender evidence. Fear and anxiety and fatigue had left him without appetite but he forced himself to eat most of the bread and drink the soup.

After the tray had been taken away, unexpectedly the light in the cell was switched off. Hurford waited until his eyes grew accustomed to the darkness, then took off the blue jacket and prison trousers and climbed into bed. The cell seemed colder than the last and both mattress and blanket were damp.

Although his body was stiff and aching with fatigue, his brain was still active, as though the fluid secreted by fear had flooded the cells and must be pumped energetically away. He realised that if he were to sleep at all, he must somehow slacken the tension of his nerves. Deliberately he put out of his mind the images of firing squads and the sound of rifle shots. With an effort of will he should be able to think about the past.

Nicole. He tried to pretend that he was lying beside her in the darkness. Outside the water was slapping the hulls of the boats in the harbour at Cannes. A door along the street opening as a drunken sailor stumbled out of a bar, released to the night six notes of Piaf's sexual moaning. Across the bay in the summer casino a thirty-year-old Cockney property millionaire was being slowly cut down to size at the Chemmy table by a syndicate of Greeks.

If he moved his hand, his fingers

would touch the warm, taut skin across Nicole's shoulders. Reaching a little further over the prominent hip-bone, he could, if he wished, cup his palm beneath one breast, lift a forefinger to gently stroke the nipple and feel it stiffen even as she slept. And there was the strange pleasure which he could always find in taking the fold of flesh around her belly between his thumb and finger, pressing it, squeezing it.

Bed with Nicole was a restful contrast to Margery's sharp, neurotic demands. It was comforting to know she was there, ready to smother waking anxiety, loneliness, the sudden pang of mortal fear, with her maternal sensuality. He drifted to sleep at last, secure in his self-deception.

When he woke not many hours later, it was with colic gripping at his stomach. For a few seconds he lay there, forgetting where he was, annoyed that he must summon the energy to walk through to their lavatory. Then he remembered and, as the pangs grew more severe, wondered what he had to do. It was the first time since his arrest that his bowels had needed relief in the night.

He stumbled across the cell in the darkness, found the door and began beating on it to attract the attention of the guards. Nobody came. His muscles, contracting till they hurt, could not hold out much longer. Then he remembered the enamel pail beneath the table. Feverishly he crossed the cell, pulled it out and squatted on it. Relief brought sweat to his temples.

Twice more during the night he woke and had to hurry to the pail. It was the food they had given him for his evening meal, he supposed, the soup in all probability, or perhaps a combination of food and the effects of fear. When finally morning came he felt worn out; physically weak and full of revulsion for the squalor of his condition. He had another hour to endure before a guard came and led him to the ablutions, where he could try to clean himself up.

After a breakfast of bread and tea — he scraped the margarine off the bread fearing that it might start another attack of diarrhoea — a guard took him upstairs to an interrogation room. Shuffling along in the laceless shoes, holding his trousers to his waist, he felt humiliated and degraded. But his anger at the Russians for treating him in this way was blunted by an increasing hopelessness. The interrogation room, number seven, was the same in which the Prosecutor's man had interviewed him before his trial by the tribunal. He knew now that he was back in the Lubianka.

Waiting in the room with the guard, he wondered what the significance of this could be. It seemed too much to believe that the authorities had relented and changed the sentence of death to imprisonment. While he was still balancing the possibilities, hope against pessimism, the Assistant Prosecutor came into the room.

"Sit down," he told Hurford.

The guard brought a wooden stool and set it in the middle of the room. Grateful, for he still felt weak after the exhaustion of the night, Hurford obeyed.

"You're lucky, Comrade Hurford," the Prosecutor said. "The sentence passed on you by the Military Tribunal has been suspended for the time being. But don't imagine that this is an act of clemency. Military Intelligence have asked for the delay in the interests of security. They wish to have confirmation of the names of those people who have been working with you against the Soviet."

All Hurford felt was a sense of enormous relief. If the sentence had been postponed there was hope. He was not even ashamed of his cowardice.

"I've already told you that no one has been working with me." He gave the answer automatically, his brain busy wondering how he could turn the situation to permanent advantage.

"Can't you see that it is absurd to persist with that story? Without some help you could not possibly have obtained the information you had in your possession when you were arrested. As a matter of fact we already know the source from which you must have obtained it."

"In that case why do you want me to tell you?"

"To confirm what we know. It would save time and inconvenience if you were to make a statement now."

"I'm sorry, no statements."

The Assistant Prosecutor came round from behind his desk and stood facing Hurford. His manner was relaxed and self-assured. Hurford began to wonder whether he might perhaps not be bluffing after all. The K.G.B. could conceivably have discovered the name of the unknown contact, Savage's precious source.

"Before you make any unwise decisions, I should tell you that I have the authority to make a deal with you. Give us a complete statement and the sentence passed on you by the Military Tribunal will be altered to a term of imprisonment."

For an instant Hurford felt a powerful temptation to agree. It would be simple to tell the Russians all he knew and the knowledge could be of little use to them. Imprisonment, even for twenty years, would be easier to endure than the walk to the firing squad. Discipline or stubbornness restrained him.

"I have nothing to add to what I have already told you."

"Why waste time with this empty bravado? In the end, as you must surely know, you'll tell everything. We have ways to make you."

"The last time I heard that threat was from the Gestapo."

"But we are not the Gestapo."

"I doubt if your methods are very different."

The Russian looked at him in disbelief. "Are you suggesting that we would use torture? No, you can't possibly be so naive! Before they sent you on this mission London must have told you about modern techniques of interrogation."

"I don't know what you're talking about."

"This is not 1944, Hurford. While you have been leading the bohemian life in the South of France, the world has moved on. We have scientific ways of extracting the truth from a prisoner; not so crude as torture and absolutely infallible."

The man was referring, Hurford supposed, to brain-washing. He had read a little about brain-washing techniques used by the Communists in the Korean war and wished now that he had learnt more about them. What concerned him more was the Prosecutor's casual remark about his life in the South of France. How much did they know about him? About the Army? About Nicole? He felt suddenly exposed and vulnerable, as though he had just met a man who admitted to having watched him in his bedroom through a two-way mirror.

The Prosecutor's man appeared to notice his uncertainty. "We know much more about you than you imagine," he said amiably, "and we can make you tell us the rest. Why don't you save all the unpleasantness by making a full statement." He turned towards the desk behind him. "See, I have a paper here. You and I can draw up a statement together for you to sign."

"I have nothing to add to what I have already told you."

"Have you not heard of the Conveyor? No? Well, it's a system of interrogation which we use for intractable cases. There's nothing physical, no torture. But after four or five days with the Conveyor, you'll be only too glad to tell us all we need to know."

23

THE Assistant Prosecutor went outside and a guard came into the room. For about twenty minutes Hurford was left alone with the man. The hard, wooden stool began to make him feel stiff and cramped, but when he stood up to stretch himself, the guard shouted at him to sit down.

Eventually a middle-aged man arrived. He had a mastiff's jaw, from which flesh hung in folds, and the watery eyes of a drunk. Sitting down at the desk, he nodded at the guard, who then left the room, and from under his arm took a file which he studied for several minutes in silence

"Well, Comrade Spy," he said at last, looking up at Hurford aggressively. "So you refuse to answer our questions?"

"I'll answer any questions that you care to ask."

"Ah, you've changed your mind, then! A very wise decision. In that case, this should not take very long." He took a piece of paper from the folder and a ball-point pen from his pocket. "All we need you to tell us is the names of your accomplices and the methods by which they passed you information."

"I had no accomplices."

"But you admit you have been engaged in espionage?"

"Certainly not."

The interrogator threw down his pen. "Didn't you say you were prepared to confess?"

"I said I would answer your questions and I am doing so."

The Russian's face twisted into a grimace which at any other time would have been comical. It could well have been an expression of resignation or despair, but the light in his eyes told Hurford it was incipient rage. He had seen the same light in the eyes of a Yugoslav partisan a moment before the man had driven a knife into the stomach of a girl, whom he suspected of having betrayed him.

"Let us understand each other." The interrogator's voice was controlled but full of menace. "My name is Krevana. In the past seventeen years I have interrogated over two thousand prisoners. Only three have failed to tell me what I wished to know. One was an old man whose heart failed even as he was sitting on that stool. The other two took their own lives."

"I can only tell you the truth. You will have to be satisfied with that."

Krevana got up and came round the desk till he was standing two feet in front of Hurford. In spite of his age and obesity, he was a powerful figure.

"The truth is exactly what you will tell me, Western swine," he said slowly. "Make no mistake, you will break down as all the others have. Now let us begin. What is your name?"

"You already know it."

"Answer when I order you," Krevana shouted.

"Michael Hurford." It would cost nothing to humour the man and talking was easier than silence. In some way it seemed to lessen the tension.

"How old are you?"

"Forty-four."

"Where were you born?"

"In England, in a town named Chesterfield."

"How long have you been in Russia?"

"Just over three months."

"And you were sent here by British Military Intelligence to spy, were you not?"

"I came as a lecturer at the British Institute."

"Do you deny that you came here to act as courier for your intelligence services, to pass back classified information?"

"Yes."

"What are your duties at the British Institute?"

"I lecture to Russian students on

163

British history, culture and literature."

"And what are your qualifications?"

"I have a degree of a British university."

"In history or literature, I assume?"

"No, modern languages."

Krevana leaned forward and stared at him triumphantly. "You admit that? So you do not have the qualifications for the post to which you were appointed?"

"I would not be qualified to lecture to adults on those subjects, it is true."

"And yet the students at the Institute are all adults."

"Only in years," Hurford replied insolently. "As one would expect after fifty years of Communist culture they have the minds of retarded children."

Without warning the Russian swung his arm wildly, his open hand catching Hurford a stinging blow on the ear. Unprepared, he fell off the stool to the ground.

"Get up!" Krevana roared.

Hurford got up slowly and faced the Russian. His hearing was distorted by a rushing noise that reminded him of times when as a child he had put sea-shells to his ear.

"You have no right to use physical violence," he said.

"Are you telling me what my rights are, filthy Fascist spy? You, son of whore, pimp for a French prostitute!"

So they did know about Nicole. The heat of anger began slowly to wrinkle the edges of Hurford's composure. It was not so much the insult or Krevana's tone that annoyed him as the knowledge that they had been spying on his past. And yet that was inevitable, given his discovery and arrest.

"I wish to complain to the Prosecutor."

"You may do so if you wish."

"Then take me to him."

"All complaints must be made in writing. You will be given pen and paper when your examination is concluded. And now sit down." Krevana pushed him towards the stool. "We will start again and this time I advise you to co-operate."

As Hurford sat down, the Russian returned to the desk, gathered his sheets of paper into a neat pile and held his pen poised.

"Tell me the name of the British intelligence organisation for which you have been working."

"I work only for the British Institute."

"Where did you obtain the photographs of classified Soviet documents that were found in your possession?"

"I never saw them until they were shown to me by the Prosecutor."

"On how many other occasions have you passed back secret information to your headquarters in London?"

"I have never passed any secret information."

"What are the names of your accomplices?"

"As I have done nothing wrong, how can I have accomplices?"

Krevana shouted: "I'll ask the questions, you piece of excrete, lecher, syphilitic protector of street girls!"

Hurford fought back his growing

anger. No doubt it was part of the Russians' tactics to make him lose his temper. That was why they had sent in this blustering oaf to bully him.

"What is the name of the British intelligence organisation for which you have been working?"

"I have already answered that question."

"Answer, you leprous dog!" Krevana screamed.

"I work only for the British Institute."

"Where did you obtain the photographs of classified Soviet documents that were found in your possession?"

"As I told you, I know nothing about them."

"On how many occasions have you passed back secret information to your headquarters in London?"

"I have passed back nothing, I tell you."

"What are the names of your accomplices? What methods did they use to contact you? How has your information been passed back to Britain?"

"I have not been engaged in spying against Russia, so I cannot answer those questions."

"Oh, you'll answer them all right, you pox-ridden capitalist. Before we finish with you, you'll tell us everything."

Krevana stared at him with gloating malevolence. Hurford found himself wondering whether the man really did hate him or whether the whole performance was histrionics. It was hard to believe that the rage and the ranting could be affected. Perhaps Krevana was a paranoic with an inbred hatred of the British whom the K.G.B. had recruited and trained as an interrogator. If so, they had miscalculated in using the man on him. It would take a more sophisticated, more devious examiner to trap him into a confession.

"What is the name of the British intelligence organisation for which you have been working?"

Krevana started on his questions

168

again and went through them, using the same words. Hurford replied as he had before, wondering how long the lunatic litany would continue. For a fourth time Krevana asked the same questions, then a fifth time and a sixth.

When for the seventh time the Russian asked the name of the intelligence organisation for which he was working, Hurford, growing tired of the endless repetition, made no reply. Krevana waited for a few seconds and then asked his remaining questions, pausing after each. When Hurford gave no answer, he did not seem disconcerted.

The interrogation continued in this style, Krevana asking the same questions time after time while his prisoner remained silent. Hurford only wondered how long the man's stamina would last. He tried counting the number of times that each question was asked but abandoned the count after twenty-four. The interrogation continued. After what must have been at least an

169

hour there was no sign that the Russian's persistence was diminishing. The monotony and the frenetic pitch of the man's voice began to eat into Hurford's patience.

Realising this, he knew also that it was the object of the interrogation. He thought, I mustn't let him get me down, mustn't weaken. There had to be a way of breaking the continuity of the performance, shaking the Russian out of his routine.

"Citizen examiner," he said suddenly and loudly. "I am prepared to make a statement."

Krevana looked at him searchingly. Prisoners, even the least resolute, did not in his experience give in so easily. But the Britisher, he knew from the notes he had been given, was an unusual type, a man of unchallenged bravery with a neurotic streak.

"So you are prepared to admit the truth?"

"I will make a statement."

"Here is paper."

"That won't be necessary. My statement is this: I work only for the British Institute, have never been engaged in spying and have no accomplices."

Krevana leapt from his desk and rushed across the room. Hurford stiffened, expecting another blow. He wondered whether he should start shouting to bring in the guard from outside. But the Russian seized him by the throat.

"What! Miserable whoremonger! You dare to be insolent? I'll have you in the punishment cells for fourteen days, then we'll see what happens to your humour."

Hurford shook himself free. Achieving this success, however small and passing, gave him enormous confidence. He knew now that nothing they could do would break him down.

"Pimp! Brothel tout!" Krevana raved. "Was it only a French girl you sold to the capitalist Jews in the South of France, or your sister as well? Maybe that was why your wife left you. You wanted to tout her to the playboys."

He went back to his desk, calling out obscenities on the way. Then almost without a pause and without concern, he restarted his examination.

"What is the name of the British intelligence organisation for which you have been working?"

"Where did you obtain the photographs of classified Soviet documents that were found in your posession?"

He went on relentlessly, asking the same questions, much more loudly now. To keep his composure, Hurford decided to ignore the noise and he concentrated on thinking about something entirely different. Not Nicole, nor Margery, for they were too close to the taunts that Krevana might at any time launch at him. He thought instead of Yugoslavia, remembering the mountain cave which had been the hideout of the partisans. He could still picture it in startling detail; the wooden crates that had served as tables, sacking hung over the entrance to screen the light of two smoking oil lamps, the box of Sten-gun ammunition parachuted down by the Air Force and wedged for safety between two rocks at the back of the cave, a sack of food that Rada had brought up from the village.

He saw Rada herself, coming up in the first light, hailing the look-out, moving slowly between the rocks, her body arched beneath the weight of the sack.

"What are the names of your accomplices? What methods did they use to contact you?"

The rough wedge of Krevana's voice thrust itself back into his consciousness. The Russian's face was mottled red with exertion and beads of sweat stretched in a row across his upper lip like a string of grey pearls.

Hurford turned his eyes away, forcing his thoughts back to the past. Rada's back was arched, under the weight not of a sack but of him. To this day he did not know why he had taken her to the clump of bushes a hundred yards from the cave. Not for one moment had he felt any lust for her. Mostly it was a gesture, that owed more than a little to adolescent recollections of Hemingway. And the outcome had been unsatisfying, with nothing of the romance of Hemingway.

"Fornicator!" He heard Krevana scream and was disconcerted by the timing of the epithet. "You could not hold your own wife, so you had to provide harlots for others. Who knows what nameless diseases are consuming your vital organs?"

For five minutes the Russian strung out his abuse. Then he returned to his aimless interrogation, as though a little obscenity had been enough to break the monotony and resharpen his zeal for his task. He came and stood in front of Hurford, bending down to stare into his prisoner's face as he screamed the questions. It was no longer possible to ignore him, to find relief in thoughts about the past. On and on went the questions, till they no longer meant anything, but assailed the senses like a mechanical noise, endlessly repetitive. And there was the repulsion of the man's face which as time went on seemed to Hurford to be gradually swelling to monstrous size, like a giant fungus jerked into animation.

Hurford felt stunned. He had to draw on all his willpower to hang on, to fight back the loathing, to resist the urge to lash out at the man.

The examination continued, stretching into time like telegraph poles beside a railway track. He did not weaken. Instead, from a hidden source, came growing strength. Gradually Krevana's harsh voice and strident questions lost their power to jar his nerves. The hatred which he had begun to feel for the man subsided and was replaced by contempt. For perhaps another twenty minutes the interrogation continued and then Hurford sensed that the Russian realised he had lost the advantage.

"You say nothing now, adulterer!" he shouted. "But before we have finished with you, you'll be begging us to let you confess." He returned to his desk and started tidying the papers in his file.

I've beaten him, Hurford thought, he's giving up. The elation which he felt was curiously emotional. He was moved like a man who had achieved an exhausting athletic triumph.

Another Russian came into the room. A tall man in a captain's uniform, he carried a small plastic bag not unlike those which airlines used to give passengers. Krevana rose from his chair.

"Thank you, Comrade Captain Lensky," he said. "I've had almost as much as I can stand of this fornicating spy."

The new man nodded. He wore spectacles with cheap metal frames which with the receding line of his soft, fair hair gave him a shy, donnish appearance. Hurford was reminded immediately of his tutor at Cambridge.

"You'll have to be firm with the whoreson, mind you," Krevana remarked as he left the room.

Hurford waited as Lensky sat down, opened a file similar to that of his predecessor and started to read the papers it contained. He seemed in no hurry to start whatever he was supposed to do.

"I'm surprised that the Soviet employs a man of that calibre to examine prisoners," Hurford said.

Lensky looked up. "What do you mean?"

"The language that he used and the childish abuse he hurled at me are a disgrace to your judicial system. And twice he lost his temper and assaulted me."

"It is not my function to discuss with you another examiner's conduct. Kindly restrain yourself."

"That is what Krevana should be told. I am strongly tempted to report his behaviour to the Prosecutor."

"Of course if that is your wish, you may do so."

"Perhaps you all will have learned at least that I am not to be bullied into submission. In the end, you see, he realised he was wasting his time."

"You surely don't believe that?" Lensky seemed genuinely surprised

"Why else has he left?"

"Citizen Krevana had been examining you for four hours. He was entitled to be relieved."

"What about me. Aren't I entitled to a break as well?"

"Oh yes, you will get a break, eventually. When you have told us all the things we need to know."

There was no threat in Lensky's tone. He seemed almost apologetic, like a mild schoolmaster who would have liked to release a pupil from detention, but must abide by the headmaster's ruling. For a moment Hurford found himself believing that the man really meant what he had said. The interrogation would continue until they broke him. Then he dismissed the idea. They would tire of this farce, he felt certain, when they realised he could not be cowed or trapped into a confession.

Lensky leant back in his chair, clasping his hands across his stomach. He looked puzzled, as though a tiny mathematical detail was preventing his solution of an otherwise straightforward problem.

"Tell me, Michael," he said persuasively. "Why are you so hostile towards the Russian people?"

Both the question and the use of his Christian name surprised Hurford. "I have nothing against the Russian people."

"We fought side-by-side with you British in the war. Nothing, no praise, was too high for us when we were your allies. Now you seek only to harm us."

"The hostility is not of our making."

"Of course it is! Has not the Soviet said time and again that she wishes only to live in peace with the world?"

"And yet you have a massive army, nuclear weapons, missiles that could obliterate our country."

"Because you have forced us to arm to defend ourselves. What is it you hate about Russia? Our people? Our way of life?"

"I keep telling you I have no personal animosity towards your country."

"Then why did you come here to spy on us?"

"I don't admit those charges."

Lensky shook his head, disappointed rather than angry with this recalcitrant pupil. "Be reasonable, Michael! Remember the evidence which we found."

"Those microdots? I know nothing about them."

"And all this equipment which was in your apartment?"

Opening the plastic holdall which he had brought with him, Lensky took out a pair of binoculars and a camera. Hurford recognised them immediately as those which had been issued to him by the Equipment Section in London.

"A pair of B.2 binoculars." Lensky held the glasses up. "Standard equipment for every intelligence agent. You know of course that they are used for reading messages transmitted in infra-red light."

Hurford was not disconcerted. He had prepared his cover story about the binoculars. They were not his property, he told the examiner, but had been left in his Moscow apartment by the previous occupier, also a lecturer at the British Institute.

"I see." Lensky sounded pleased that he had been able to explain the binoculars. "And the camera?"

"That camera's mine all right. But what's wrong with that? Lots of people take cameras with them when they go abroad."

The Russian captain opened the back of the camera, looked inside, then turned it round and stared at the lens. "But this is no ordinary camera. It would be valueless for taking ordinary snapshots or tourist views. Our experts tell me it is fitted with a revolutionary lens, only recently developed in America. It enables one to make minutely small reproductions without the aid of any other optical instrument. Its only practical value is for the spy who wished to make microdots."

Hurford hesitated fractionally, then improvised: "In that case the lens must have been fitted by someone else."

The answer was transparently unconvincing and he could only hope that his tone was not the same. He remembered what Fossick had told him back in London about the camera. Could they have blundered in the Equipment Section and issued him with the wrong instrument? Since he had been in Moscow he had never tried to use it.

"I wish I could convince you," he told Lensky, "that I didn't come here to spy."

"Let's not talk about that. We'll

return to what I was saying before about the hostility of the West towards Russia. The sight of this camera reminds me of a point to illustrate what I mean. Every year thousands of British and American tourists visit Moscow and what is it they want to photograph? Our great buildings? Our monuments? Our parks and theatres? No. Only the few old-fashioned houses that still exist in the back streets."

"Your slums."

"All right, if you wish to use emotive words, our slums. Tell me, why is that, except through hostility?"

"Because you try to hide them. Tourists are carefully kept away."

"And why not? If you invite a man to your home do you show him the small, dark bedroom which you cannot afford to furnish? Do you point out the patch of peeling paintwork? Do you open the cupboard full of junk?"

"No, that's a fair point," Hurford admitted. He was pleasantly surprised by the line of argument Lensky was following and had no objections to sitting there all day discussing abstract political propositions, even though he could not understand what the examination was supposed to achieve.

"We are proud of our achievements," Lensky continued. "Only fifty years ago Russia was the most backward country in Europe. We had no industry to speak of, no technology and a population of oppressed and illiterate peasants. Today we are winning the race of space exploration and we lead the world in science, medicine, applied art."

"That may be partly true, but your achievements have been at the expense of personal liberty. You have deprived the people of their freedom."

"That is your opinion. Freedom, like all abstractions, is relative. We Russians have as much freedom as we need."

"Ah, yes! The freedom not only to live but to die in one of Stalin's purges."

Lensky rose from his desk, turned

away and looked out of the window thoughtfully, as though he needed time to consider this cynical innuendo. Hurford could not help being attracted to the man. In different circumstances they might have been friends. Men like Lensky, self-effacing intellectuals, unsuccessful writers and artists, had formed the small circle of their friends in Cannes. Drifters, lotus-eaters, perhaps, but reasonable people.

"Think for a moment, Michael. As a young man, at school and university, did you never hold progressive ideas?"

"Certainly. By the time I was eighteen I had been a Fabian, a Communist, an anarchist and a pacifist."

"Then have you no sympathy for our ideals?"

"For your ideals in 1917 I have every sympathy, but not for the methods you adopted in pursuit of them. You did not attain equality and freedom, you debased them."

The argument flowed on, for an hour or more, murmuring its way through

185

history and political science. Much of what the Russian said was difficult to refute, for he was a persuasive speaker who had the advantage of knowing not only his own case but that of his opponent. Hurford realised he was being out-manœuvred but he had never resented being beaten in debate. He had few intellectual pretensions and no competitive spirit.

A guard came into the room carrying a tray with a pot of tea and sandwiches, which he placed on the desk in front of Lensky. Seeing the food, Hurford was suddenly aware of a compelling hunger. The rations which had been given to him for the past week were no more than the bare minimum necessary for life, and the purging of the previous night had sharpened his appetite.

"Why are your questioning me about politics?" he asked the examiner.

"Because I wish to understand you."

"I'm sure your superiors would expect something more positive."

"Nothing can be more positive than

186

learning to understand a man," the Russian said. He poured himself a cup of tea as he ate one of the sandwiches. "When I understand you, then I will also know the motives which made you work against our country. And so I will be able to persuade you to give me the information we require."

"How?"

"By showing you how wrong you have been. You are not a man to refuse an appeal to his conscience."

"Conscience? Me? An old soldier and an unsuccessful teacher? You're joking!"

Lensky smiled. "We shall see. In the meantime, have one of these sandwiches."

"No thank you."

"You see, you are a man of principles!" Lensky said jovially. "You do not want to eat my food in case that puts you under an obligation to me. In other words, you have a conscience."

"Perhaps I have," Hurford replied. "I'm beginning to feel guilty because

I'm wasting your time."

"My time is not so important."

"But you'll never get a confession from me and that's what your chiefs will expect."

"We'll get it all right." Lensky stopped smiling and looked depressed. "I wish I could persuade you to realise that, Michael. It would be so much better for you if you were sensible now and talked the matter over frankly. I'm not thinking of myself."

"Don't you understand? I'll never admit to your charges."

"Of course you will. No one has ever beaten the Conveyor."

"What is this Conveyor everyone talks about?"

"I wish I could explain what it is and what you are letting yourself in for, but that's not my duty. Anyway you'll know soon enough."

Hurford wondered for how long they had been talking. He could tell from the failing light outside that night was approaching. The stool on which he was sitting had begun to cause him acute discomfort. With no support for his back, he had to sit erect and the sharp edge of the seat was cutting into his flesh.

"Will it be all right if I stand up for a few minutes, Citizen Examiner?"

"That is not permitted, I'm afraid."

"Why on earth not?"

"Those are the rules of the interrogation. Prisoners must remain seated."

"In that case I should like your permission to go to the lavatory."

"You will have an opportunity for that in due course, but not now."

"That's absurd! And inhuman! Where is this justice you were talking about so eloquently?"

Lensky hesitated. "I'll allow you to stand but only for two minutes. And make the most of it, because it won't happen again."

The man was kind-hearted it was obvious. The knowledge should have filled Hurford with contempt for an opponent's weakness and satisfaction because this was a weakness he could exploit. Instead he felt sorry for Lensky. In Russia, as anywhere else, a man could drift into a job for which he was totally unsuited.

He got up from the stool and walked a few steps, flexing his muscles. Lensky watched anxiously, as though he were afraid one of the guards might come in and discover this breach of regulations. Hurford found himself almost wishing he could give him something in return.

"I wish I could explain how that camera was tampered with," he said lamely. "But I just don't know."

"Don't worry about that. It's not important."

"Perhaps it isn't my camera after all. I could have picked it up somewhere, mistaking it for mine."

"You must sit down now," the Russian said. "It's almost time for me to leave."

Hurford returned to the stool. "What happens now?"

"The examination will be continued

by Comrade Nina Ilyana."

"A woman? You use women in this job?"

"Why not? Nina is one of our most able examiners."

"Able or not, she is unlikely to make any more progress than you."

"But I've made excellent progress." Lensky smiled shyly. "Our talk has been very instructive."

Again Hurford could not help but like the man. It was hard to see how the Russian was going to last long in a job like this. He remarked flippantly: "I'm glad I've been a satisfactory pupil."

"But how much better if you were to save everyone's time and tell us all we want to know."

"Sorry, there's no hope of that."

Lensky picked up the telephone on the desk and said into it: "Tell the Comrade Examiner I am ready." Within a few seconds the door opened and a woman came into the room. It happened so quickly that she must have been waiting outside the door.

"Thank you, Nina Ilyana, for relieving me so promptly."

"I daresay you're ready for a break. They tell me the prisoner is being particularly difficult."

Lensky left the room and she took his place at the desk. She was a woman of about forty totally lacking in any form of distinction. Her face was plain, without make-up, and her skin gave the impression of being grey to match the dull grey dress she was wearing. It seemed impossible to believe that she could ever laugh, cry, express anger, grief or passion. Hurford could see that she might be industrious and efficient, but the overriding impression which she gave was of anonymity.

"I hope you are prepared to be helpful," she opened by saying. "That will make things much more pleasant for both of us."

"If by helpful you mean that I should confess to the ridiculous accusations which have been made against me, then the answer is no."

"I am not here to discuss your offences against the Soviet."

"Then what?"

"We would like to know more about your education and attainments. What you did in the Army for example."

"My army career is past history," Hurford replied. "There is nothing I can tell you now which would be of any value to your Intelligence."

"It is not British secrets that interest me."

"Ah, I know! Like your colleague, Lensky, you want only to understand me."

Nina Ilyana ignored his sarcasm. "Are you willing to answer my questions?"

The correct attitude, Hurford reflected, would have been to tell her nothing except his name. By keeping silent one could not inadvertently give anything away. But he had found with Krevana that silence in the face of incessant questioning was exhausting. He was confident that he could frame his replies with care, avoiding any traps. As long as the interrogators continued with the absurd charade of playing the psychiatrist or father confessor, he would play along with them.

"Provided you confine yourself to questions about my past, I'll answer them."

"Tell me about your school, then. You went to school in Chesterfield, I believe?"

"Yes. First to a primary school for children up to the age of eleven and then to a grammar school."

"And were you sent away from your home?"

"I didn't go to boarding schools, if that's what you mean."

"But the schools were for boys only?"

"The primary school was mixed; the grammar school for boys alone."

"Do you think it is a good idea to segregate the sexes in education?"

"I've never thought about it very much. No doubt there is something to be said for both points of view."

Nina Ilyana made a note in her file. "Didn't you find that being deprived in adolescence of female company induced certain frustrations?"

"No, I don't think so."

"Psychiatrists agree it is bad to herd men together," the Russian persisted. She appeared determined to make a point. "Even in the Army it is bad. Our Supreme Army Council is much concerned with this problem."

"Well, I don't believe it did me any harm."

"Perhaps you were not aware of it. But think, did you never have any experiences which subsequently you came to regret?"

Suddenly Hurford realised what the woman was implying. He laughed. "I'm not a homosexual, if that's what you imagine."

"A great many Englishmen are."

"That's just one of those myths which your propaganda boys have invented. No doubt there is just as much perversion in Russia. Otherwise your

Army Council would not be worried by the problem."

"We will not start an argument. It is you I am interested in, not British morality."

Hurford decided that he had scored a valuable point. The woman was not nearly so skilled a debater as Lensky. If it had not been for the growing discomfort that sitting on the stool was causing him, he would have been ready to enjoy this confrontation.

"So you say you have never experienced sexual problems?" Nina Ilyana said.

"Sex has never been an obsession with me."

"Ah, that is a different matter!"

"If that's not what you meant, what kind of problems had you in mind?"

"You were living away from your wife. There must have been reasons for the break-up of your marriage."

"They weren't sexual."

"No? And you had no children?"

"My wife's maternal instincts were

not very strong. Night life was more in her line than nappies."

"You are still bitter!" The Russian appeared pleased.

"Not at all. Our separation was all handled in a civilised way."

"But that doesn't answer my question. Why did your marriage fail?"

"The Americans would say through incompatibility," Hurford answered without hesitation. He had given the convenient explanation so often before that he had come to accept it, even though he did not believe it. "But so many wartime marriages foundered in the same way that I suppose outside factors must have played a part."

"What factors?"

"The transition from war to peace was one. It was not only men who found it difficult to adjust themselves to the routine of ordinary life after the excitement of war."

This was at least partly true. He recalled Margery's boredom in the aimless days after the Japanese had surrendered.

How she had hated the bungalow they had rented when he was on a staff course at Camberley. The conflict of war had for them been replaced by petty skirmishes of domesticity. She had bullied him into living beyond their income, nagging him to repeated visits to London. Almost the only times she had been happy were when they met friends in the Café Royal, drank too much gin, danced at Hatchetts, spinning out the evenings with army gossip.

"You believe your relationship with your wife was perfectly satisfactory?" Nina Ilyana asked.

"Until the war ended, yes," Hurford replied, thinking that it was no more than a semblance of a lie. "Afterwards, for the reasons I've explained, we began to drift apart."

The Russian woman glanced down at the papers in front of her. "And not very long after your wife left you,

you went to live in France. Why was that?"

"After leaving the Army, I had to get other work. I tried various jobs, but none of them seemed to suit me. So I drifted into teaching."

"But why in France?"

"It enabled me to use my languages."

"Are you sure it was not because in France there is much more sexual freedom? After all, you chose to work in a girls' school."

"Oh, for God's sake!" Hurford protested. "Surely you're not going to find a deep motive in that? Why do you persist in treating me like a sexual acrobat?"

"No man who spies can be wholly normal," she replied tartly.

Hurford laughed, but the interrogation was beginning to irritate him. With her ceaseless probing, her obsession with sex, the Russian woman reminded him of a Girton girl he had known at Cambridge, who had thrust her company on him, exploiting his easy nature. After three weeks any sympathy he might have felt for her had turned first into distaste and then into hatred.

"Perhaps your French mistress was able to give you more than your wife."

"You have no reason for thinking that."

"You stayed with her for four years."

"I stayed with my wife for more than fourteen."

"But you were married to her."

"I still am. And in the end, as you know, I left the French girl as well."

Nina Ilyana looked at him intently as though she expected his next words to give her the ultimate clue to his behaviour. "Yes. You left your easy, bohemian life among the decadent French. I wonder why? The call of duty? How do you say it in England? For King and country?"

"I left because they sacked me from my job."

"Because you had improper relations with one of the small girls."

So they knew even that. The discovery

did not wholly surprise him, but he felt for the first time since his arrest a sense of helplessness. The Russian machine was programmed, fully activated, entirely efficient. How could anyone hope to resist it?

"You know everything," he said roughly. "So you must know that was untrue, a false accusation."

"Very probably. It was no doubt the cover London provided for you. After all why should you need sex with little girls, if you were so happy with your mistress? Unless of course one woman is not enough to satisfy you. That could also have been the reason why your wife left you."

Hurford stared at her incredulously. "What are you suggesting?"

"That she could no longer put up with your excessive sexual demands."

"Mine? You're joking!" He laughed out loud. There was satisfaction and relief in the laughter, because she was so wide of the truth. Without any deception he had deceived her. She was a victim of her artlessness, of a spinster's delusion that only men were over-sexed. Once again, he decided, he had outwitted her.

For a few moments the Russian bent over the desk, making notes busily. She asked her next question without looking up from her papers. "Did you know that the French girl has taken another man?"

"How do you know?"

"A red-headed American painter named Ivens. Like you he left his wife to go and live in France, but he is young."

"Unlike me, you mean. I didn't know that, but it does not astonish me."

"Why not?"

"A girl has to live and Nicole does not like working."

"Surely you're jealous that she has taken another lover?" the Russian asked.

"No."

"You don't mind at all?"

He was about to say that he did not mind, when the denial was cut short by a startling picture. He saw Nicole on the bed, their bed, with her strands of hair black serpents across the sheet. Over her crouched the lean, young American, carrot hair, athletic hips.

"I'm still fond of Nicole, but one has to be reasonable. She lived with me for four years. She could scarcely be expected to live alone for long."

"Ah, you're saying she would need a man."

"Yes," Hurford answered carelessly.

"Is she then a nymphomaniac?"

"Good God, no!"

"Her sexual desires were quite normal?"

The Russian stared at him again, waiting for his answer. He seemed to detect in her manner an expectancy that was almost obscene. This was the only way she could enjoy sex, vicariously, since she was too unattractive to find a man.

"I really don't see why I should

answer a question like that."

"Why should you mind? The woman is nothing to you now?"

"But she was once."

"Please Mister Hurford." She used the English title, mocking him. "Forget your outmoded British chivalry. You are not an officer any more, but a bohemian, an intellectual. Let us have a little intellectual frankness."

Replying was easier than arguing. "There was nothing abnormal about Nicole."

The Russian woman continued interrogating him, quickening the pace, with a succession of questions that had only the most tenuous connection, except that all were on some aspect of his marriage or of sex. Hurford found his concentration weakening and he answered her carelessly, with a diminishing attention to accuracy or truth. Through the window of the room he had noticed night fall and it had been dark now for an hour or more. He had been in the room the whole day and was aware now of an immense weariness. His buttocks and thighs were being slowly seized into painful rigidity. Wriggling on the stool to change his position no longer brought any relief. He would have asked Nina Ilyana if he could stand up for a short time, but intuition told him she was not a woman who would grant favours graciously.

You can stick it out a little longer, he told himself, they must give you a break soon.

He continued to answer her questions almost mechanically, leaving a part of his mind free to think about discomfort. And then the break came, sooner than he expected. Abruptly without warning, the Russian woman gathered her papers together. Then she picked up the telephone.

"Take number seven down to the cells," she said into the instrument.

"Is the interrogation over?" Hurford asked.

"It is time for your evening meal."

A guard came in to take him away. As he walked downstairs to the ablutions, Hurford enjoyed a feeling of elation. He had seen the day through, proved that his powers of endurance were equal to the test. Next day, no doubt, there would be more questions, perhaps a more searching interrogation, with the same to follow for days to come. But he was certain now that he could survive any examination they might devise.

From the ablutions he was taken back to his cell and another guard brought in his evening meal. The soup had a few small pieces of sausage floating in it. The tea was bitter but he drank it, thinking he would need every ounce of nourishment to sustain him.

After eating, he lay down on his bed and only then did he really become aware of his exhaustion. Every muscle of his body, arms and legs seemed to throb with pain. To ease the stiffness of his thighs and buttocks, he lay on his stomach. Almost immediately his sense began to spiral downwards towards sleep. Time was suspended and his thoughts frozen in the last image of consciousness. It was the fate of the examiner, Krevana, fixed in a cataleptic grimace of rage.

But before the image was finally extinguished, he felt himself being shaken. Stupidly he stared through closing eyes at the guard who stood by the bed.

"Get up!" the man shouted. "On your feet!"

"What is it?"

"I have to take you back for interrogation."

24

IN room number seven Krevana sat waiting for him. The Russian looked composed, affable and expectant, as though he were about to meet an old and well-liked friend. The guard led Hurford to the stool and went out leaving them alone.

"Did you enjoy your meal?" Krevana asked.

"Not very much. But then you would not expect me to."

"All this loose living in the South of France has made you soft. A man's body needs discipline."

Hurford could not help thinking that it was Krevana who needed physical discipline. Although the man was powerfully built, he was bordering on the obese, like a superannuated wrestler.

"You could be back in France,"

Krevana continued. "Back in the arms of your mistress. All you have to do is make a statement."

"I've told you all I know."

"We shall find out in due course whether you have. But let us proceed. I don't want to detain you any longer than necessary." The Russian bellowed at this humorous shaft and glanced down at his notes, like an actor taking a last look at his lines. "First tell me the name of the British Intelligence organisation for which you have been working."

"I work only for the British Institute in Moscow."

"How foolish you are to persist in these lies. You would be telling us nothing we do not already know."

"Then why have you asked me that question more than a hundred times?"

Krevana made a show of seeming incredulous. "You think we do not know? About your chief Colonel Fenton and the man Savage who was with you in the Army?" He laughed, enjoying

Hurford's momentary surprise. "We know all that and more. We know it was your Equipment Section which supplied you with this, for example."

From a drawer in the desk he produced, with a quick flourish, the radio set that Hurford had found in his apartment when he had arrived in Moscow. The set had a telescopic VHF aerial and Kevana drew it out, till it was fully extended.

"Another piece of standard British Intelligence equipment. Shall we tune in to your private frequency? But no, they would be transmitting some innocent programme, I suppose. Only you know at what times the special coded broadcasts are made."

"Sometimes I really believe this is a gigantic hoax." Hurford spoke slowly, playing for time and wondering what further shocks the Russian might hold for him. The interrogation had started badly, putting him already at a disadvantage. "I can't even begin to understand what you are talking about.

You must have arrested me in mistake for someone else."

"And where did you obtain the photographs of classified documents that were found in your possession?"

"Didn't you know? They were planted on me by one of your K.G.B. stooges."

"What! You dare to suggest that a member of our organisation would ever be guilty of such conduct?"

"Why not? The good Soviet citizen can no longer distinguish between truth and falsehood. He is not allowed to."

"Bastard!" Krevana shouted. "Capitalist excrete! One more word and I'll have you in the punishment cells."

"There you are! Under the Soviet code, it is an offence even to speak one's mind." Hurford taunted the Russian recklessly. A day or two in the punishment cells was beginning to seem more attractive than four hours with Krevana.

The Russian screamed some unintelligible abuse, picked up a brass paperweight from the desk and hurled it at his prisoner. It flew past Hurford's head and dented the plaster on the wall behind before clattering to the floor.

"This time you've gone too far! The Prison Commissar shall hear of your behaviour." Hurford smiled insolently and the Russian, almost hysterical with anger continued: "On how many occasions, fascist beast, have you passed back secret information to your chiefs in London?"

He lapsed into his catechism of questions, as though they might exorcise his own violence. "What are the names of your accomplices in Russia? What methods have you been using to contact them?"

Inexhaustible, the Russian went on, repeating each question almost as loudly as he could and with the same inflexions every time. Hurford answered, precisely at first, choosing his words. But after an hour or more the sheer monotony began to chafe his senses and distract him from what he was saying. Krevana's voice was having the same effect as the pop music to which Nicole used to listen for hours at a time on the transistor radio. He had been unwise enough to buy her the radio and it was his insolence which had prised the stopper of Krevana's self-control. In the previous session with the Russian, he had been able for long periods to ignore Krevana's strident bullying. Now he found it impossible to blot out the face or the voice by diverting his thoughts elsewhere.

He thought suddenly, it'll drive me round the bend, I'll have to shout at him, strangle that bloody voice out of his throat. The idea frightened him. There was a line beyond which he dare not allow himself to be pushed. Violence hovered there, with its lining of lunacy and he flinched from it.

Before the struggle for restraint began, providence came to his help as it so often did. Inexplicably, Krevana changed his tactics.

"Is it true you're a Catholic?"

213

"Yes."

"And what do the priests think about your lechery?" Krevana demanded. "Did you go running to them from your mistress's bed? Did they forgive you your adultery?"

"Citizen Examiner, I feel I should warn you that you're only wasting your time with this childish rubbish."

"Insolent dog! Before we've finished with you your stubborn pride will be broken."

"Don't be too confident about that."

"Ah, you think because you resisted the Gestapo that you can outwit us."

"Why not? The fascist mentality is very much the same everywhere."

Krevana leapt to his feet. "Filthy son of a bitch! You dare to compare us with the Germans?"

"There are many similarities. Your methods, your mentality, your ideology."

The Russian began to swear and shout. Watching him, however, Hurford had the impression that there was at least as much performance as passion

214

in the display. It was as though Krevana felt obliged from time to time to raise the emotional level of the interrogation. The intention could well have been to exhaust a prisoner by sapping his nervous energy. Hurford decided he would not allow it to succeed with him.

"Scab! Syphilitic scab!" Krevana shouted. "Tell me at once the names of your accomplices, British spy, or it will be the worse for you. What methods have you been using to contact them?"

The questions started again. The words, the gestures, the grimaces had become grotesque in their familiarity. The rasping voice ranted on.

You must fight it, Hurford told himself, don't let him weaken you. He'll tire first.

In an attempt to isolate his mind from the frightening monotony, the noise, he began reciting to himself English poems. 'Bright Star would I were steadfast as thou art', and 'You meaner beauties of the night'; all the poems of darkness and tranquillity that he could remember.

By contrast the single lamp in the room threw a sickly, nervous brightness. With all windows closed, the air was warm and fetid. This was the room, Hurford supposed, where countless men had been persecuted; the forgotten anonymous millions who had been sacrificed in Stalin's purges; the political prisoners whose only offence was an unguarded word or a neighbour's accusation. Here while Moscow slept, their minds had been slowly and systematically crushed into craven docility.

Time and the meaningless questions rolled on endlessly, till he wished desperately that the interrogation would finish. That would not be the end, of course. Lensky was probably already standing by, reading from his notes, framing his questions. But a session with Lensky would be pleasant by comparison with Krevana's violence.

There was every chance, too, that Lensky would allow him to stand and ease his tortured muscles. The pain in his thighs and his groin was becoming difficult to endure. He found himself looking forward to the time when Lensky would let him rise and walk about and began savouring the relief it would bring.

At last the questions stopped and Krevana showed he had concluded by collecting his papers together on the desk. He picked up the telephone and for one ecstatic moment Hurford thought he was going to call for a guard to take him back to his cell. Instead he said curtly: "Tell the Citizen Examiner I have finished my interrogation."

When the door opened and Nina Ilyana came into the room, Hurford recoiled before his disappointment. He could expect no favours from Nina. Like most women in positions of authority she would carry out her duty conscientiously and without pity. As though to confirm this assessment, she wasted no time and asked her first question before Krevana had even left the room.

"I intend to recapitulate on part of our discussion this afternoon. I am especially interested in your wife. How long is it since you saw her last?"

"Why can't my wife be left out of this? Nothing she ever did has any bearing on the charges you have made against me."

"Be kind enough to answer my questions."

Hurford was too weary to argue. He would reply, but not truthfully to find out how much the K.G.B. knew. "About eight years."

"Has she married again?"

"We have never been divorced."

"Why did you never have any children?"

"Perhaps my wife was barren."

"Earlier you said it was because she had no maternal instinct."

"What on earth does it matter?"

Hurford was irritated because through carelessness he had slipped into what she might think was a clever trap.

"No, it's not important. There are other matters we should discuss. Tell me, how old was the French girl, your mistress?"

She began then to ask him questions about Nicole's appearance, habits, character, education and upbringing. The questions were so far removed from espionage or intelligence that Hurford decided she could only be asking them to satisfy her own erotic curiosity.

For himself, talking about Nicole brought back poignant memories. In a series of images he saw and relived the best moments of their association: the drowsy waking to Sunday mornings, love in a cool room when the afternoon sun fixed red roofs and pink walls in shimmering immobility, walking back arm-in-arm and a little tipsy from the café, the sudden unexpected caress, silence unimpoverished by words.

Remembering Nicole, he felt the beginnings of lust for her.

"Did you ever undergo psychiatric treatment?" he heard the Russian woman ask.

"No. Why should I?"

"Obviously your preoccupation with sex is unnatural. You should have been given treatment."

He had the guilty feeling that she had been eavesdropping on his lecherous thoughts of Nicole. Could the Russians have even devised a way of bugging a man's mind? He blustered: "What the hell are you talking about?"

"Your unnatural appetite for sex."

"Mine?"

"Certainly. You must have realised it because it is obvious to everyone. Why, my fellow examiners even cautioned me against interrogating you alone in this room."

Hurford stared at her incredulously. With her plain face, dumpy figure and drab clothes, it was inconceivable that she could ever imagine herself to be in danger from a man. He told her with exaggerated politeness: "Please don't think me ungallant, Citizen Examiner, but to be frank you don't attract me in that way."

"It is easy to say that. Even though you do not like me, your sexual urges are so strong . . . " She left the sentence unfinished, rose from the desk and walked round in front of it till she stood opposite him.

Good God, Hurford thought, she's going to make some sort of advances, try to seduce me. The idea was so preposterous, that he could not suppress a laugh.

"I am no longer young," Nina Ilyana said slowly. "I am not pretty. But do you deny that you would have sex with me if there was an opportunity?"

"Sorry to disappoint you, but I wouldn't under any circumstances."

She moved nearer him, turned sideways and gathered her dress in tightly at the waist to show off her figure.

Her breasts were fuller than they appeared, but there was nothing else to commend her; her legs were thick and shapeless and covered with hair, her hips disproportionately large. She started to undo the zip at the back of her dress. Then she pulled one sleeve down till it revealed a shoulder. The whole performance was a ludicrous caricature of a striptease.

"Well?" she demanded. "Do you still deny it?"

The sexual stirring that Hurford had felt when thinking of Nicole still lingered. Incredibly, it did not diminish, but grotesque and distasteful though the Russian woman was, seemed to grow stronger. The discovery shocked him. It was surely impossible to feel any lust for her.

"Come now. Admit it!" Nina Ilyana persisted.

"Don't be ridiculous!"

Swiftly, before he could check her, she bent down and thrust her hand into his groin.

"Ah, I knew it!" Her voice was triumphant but she gave no other sign of pleasure. "Our assessment of you is correct. Sexually you're insatiable."

Angry and humiliated, he pushed her away. To argue with her would only shame him more because she would not believe him. He felt degraded, a small boy detected in a dirty act.

Buttoning up her dress, Nina Ilyana returned to her desk and made more notes. Seeing her record her spurious observations only increased Hurford's anger. Now his humiliation would be exposed for others to see.

"Tell me, at what age did you have your first sexual experience?" the Russian woman asked calmly.

He was tempted to shout abuse at her, to let her feel the lash of his tongue and so return some of the mortification she had inflicted on him. But he realised it would be wasted effort and bad tactics, only weakening his position further.

"I must have been five," he replied,

turning instead to sarcasm. "Or perhaps four."

"That's impossible."

"Oh, no, I can assure you! With my nanny's little daughter. Of course I won't claim it was a particularly mature sensation."

"A child of that age would not even know about such things."

"Not in Russia, perhaps, but as you must realise, the West is decadent. Haven't you read Aldous Huxley? My nurse encouraged this sex play. It kept me occupied and out of mischief."

He saw her hesitate between scepticism and wonder. Then, either to conceal her indecision or through a sense of duty, she made a note of his reply. The fact that he had turned the tables on her helped to ease his bruised pride, even if it did not lessen his sense of shame.

As she continued with the examination, he wondered how he could possibly have felt the sharp pang of lust which still assailed him. Only too well he knew that her remarks about his sexual appetite were unfounded. Even admitting that some months had passed since he had slept with a woman, frustration alone could not account for a feeling which seemed so unnatural. Even when he was drunk, there was always a certain fastidiousness which made him selective. Could it be a symptom of emotional stress, he wondered, or some twisted manifestation of fear?

His speculation was suddenly interrupted by a spasm of pain. Shifting on the seat to ease it, he became aware that his whole body in the region of his thighs and groin was aching. Even the mere act of sitting on the stool required a physical effort and his abdomen and groin appeared to have swollen. The temptation to stand up, risking a rebuke or even punishment, grew stronger.

For a time he toyed with the idea of pretending to faint so he could fall from the stool to the ground. To lie for even a few moments on the floor must bring relief to the excruciating pain. Then he remembered that this was what the Russian wanted: to drive him first to physical submission and from that to a confession.

He must hang on, defy them. Pain could be endured if one knew the secret. He remembered the crude, sustained torture of the Gestapo. One needed intense concentration, not on distracting thoughts, but on the pain itself. In this way one could recognise it, explore it, understand it, till the act of bearing the pain was no longer an end in itself but incidental to a broader experience. After a time the pain became a part of consciousness and, inexplicably, almost a source of pleasure.

Today the method worked only partially. With her incessant questions the Russian woman kept pulling his attention back to her.

"Did you never feel ashamed, as a child, of these sexual urges?"

Morning came. Through the window he saw the first grey light gradually etch in the outlines of surrounding buildings. The skyscraper tower of an hotel or government building chased the last strands of night away like an admonishing finger.

At last it was over. When Nina Ilyana's hand reached for the telephone, he was too tired to feel any pleasure in his achievement. Apart from the hideous pain in his stomach and buttocks, his mind was numb with weariness and could no longer recognise any sense of relief. In any case he had nothing to look forward to except the lenience of Lensky.

"Take number seven down."

The unexpectedness of her instructions shook him from his apathy. Even though he knew the ordeal was not over, the prospect of even a temporary relief, of being allowed to walk to the ablutions, of five minutes of solitude in his cell, filled him with almost insupportable happiness. When the guard came, he wanted to show his gratitude to Nina Ilyana.

"Thank you Citizen Examiner," he said and stumbled stiffly out of the room.

25

"WHY won't you accept the truth, Michael?" Lensky asked. "In the end you'll have to tell us what we want to know. Do it now and spare yourself this unpleasant business."

He looked clean and freshly shaven, ready and inexhaustible. This was not surprising for while Hurford had fought with Krevana and writhed under Ilyana, Lensky had been home, eaten, slept and played with his two small boys.

When he had been brought back to the interrogation room, Hurford had still felt confident in his ability to resist. Ten minutes in the ablutions, a quick breakfast taken standing up and a few moments lying face down on his bed had eased his aching muscles. Refreshed, he knew he was equal to anything the Conveyor could attempt.

But now, seeing Lensky, his optimism slid away like sand in an hour glass, leaving a growing void.

"We already know almost everything."

"You're bluffing!"

Lensky looked hurt. "All right. Then tell me, why did you accept the post at the British Institute?"

"Because I needed a job."

"Why?"

"I was dismissed from the school where I was teaching."

"There! That's just an example of how stupid you are to try to deceive us. We know the story is only part of your cover."

"I don't know what you mean."

"The facts are these." Lensky glanced at his notes. "You were supposed to be dismissed for having an unhealthy relationship with a pupil, Monique Lesage. The charge was completely false."

"Of course it was."

"Yes. And yet the girl's father brought pressure on the headmaster to dismiss you. Why?"

"I've no idea."

"Come, Michael, we are not children. We made our investigations. The girl's uncle arranged everything. He is a top official in the French Government. Of course he did it at the request of British Intelligence."

Dimly Hurford thought, this is all part of a trap, but what's the point of it? Fatigue and cumulative effect of twenty-four hours of interrogation had left him confused. Suspicious and uncertain, he decided to say nothing.

"You're an intelligent fellow. Surely you can see that this stubborn pretence is useless. Admit your offences. You'll find Russia is magnanimous."

Hurford's defiant laugh was a tired croak. Already the pain had returned and his whole body below the waist began to burn as though held over a fire.

Skilfully Lensky elaborated his theme. The Soviet did not believe in wasting the most precious of resources, human talent. If Hurford admitted his errors and co-operated, the past could be erased. They would find a role for him in the work of reorganising Europe.

Listening, Hurford could not understand how he had ever believed that Lensky's examination was more bearable than that of his two colleagues. The appeal of logic was difficult to counter and the Russian's sincerity had begun to make indefinable demands on him.

Somehow he lasted the long four hours. Krevana came next and began his stint with every appearance of sadistic pleasure. As he shouted his empty questions, Hurford found himself thinking about what Lensky had said. Had his dismissal from the French school really been contrived. The idea was absurd. Why should the French Government be involved? Besides he seemed to recall that Savage had not approached him until after he had been sacked. Or was that true? His brain was finding it difficult to select memories and place them in an orderly sequence. Which was cause and which effect? He could no longer be certain. As the interrogation continued, the past and the present, his memories and the statements of the examiners, slowly became fused into a hideous dream.

Early in the afternoon Krevana was relieved by Nina Ilyana. With a painful effort Hurford calculated that they had been interrogating him without interruption for almost thirty hours. He knew too that they would continue. The examiners were trained, tough and determined. Questions, arguments, the agony of sitting on the stool stretched out before him into time. The prospect was harder to bear than the ordeal itself. If there had been an ending to look forward to, a time limit, he could have disciplined himself to survive. As it was, he was filled with a sense of hopelessness.

By the middle of that night, the pain in his thighs was unbearable. More than anything he wished he could pass out. Then they would have to suspend the interrogation. God let me faint, let me collapse, he prayed.

Krevana shouted across the room: "On how many other occasions did you pass back secret information to British Intelligence?"

In desperation, Hurford resorted to the plan which he had rejected earlier in the day. With an exaggerated groan he slipped from the stool on to the floor and lay there.

Krevana's reaction was different from what he had expected. The Russian showed no sign of alarm or even concern. He rose, came round to the front of the desk and looked down at Hurford calmly. "Get back on that stool at once," he ordered. When Hurford only groaned, he kicked him sharply but not violently in the chest. "Don't waste time shamming. You can't deceive us. It's all been tried by prisoners before."

"I refuse," Hurford replied. "You

can question me as I lie here."

"If you're not back on the stool in fifteen seconds, I'll send for a strait-jacket. If necessary we'll strap you to your seat."

Hurford ignored the threat until it was repeated, emphasised by another kick in the stomach. Then, recognising defeat, he hauled himself slowly back on to the stool. The diversion had been worthwhile. Even two minutes of relief from the torture of sitting had been a delicious sensation.

Early next morning he found himself staring through swollen eyes at Nina Ilyana. The Russian woman's attitude towards him had changed perceptibly. The questions, the argument remained much the same but her disdain for him kept breaking through like an ill-disciplined trombone in a colliery band. Believing that he had wanted her physically, instead of softening her, appeared to have given her a sense of superiority.

Then to Hurford's surprise she

turned without warning to an entirely different approach.

"Since last night I have discussed your case with our psychiatrist. Now we understand the subconscious impulses which drove you to your discreditable actions. It would be better if you understood them yourself."

"What fantasy has your witch doctor concocted this time?"

"You will find us sympathetic." Nina Ilyana ignored his taunt. "After all none of us is responsible for his biological make-up. It is especially difficult for a man who finds he is sexually inadequate."

"A few hours ago I was a sexual maniac, now I'm impotent."

"Not impotent, inadequate."

"You astonish me." With sarcasm, Hurford could restrain the anger which threatened to ignite. "Aren't I the man who was so over-sexed that he even lusted over you?"

"That was just an experiment," Nina Ilyana said coldly. "You were given an aphrodisiac in your food."

Hurford remembered the bitter taste of the tea served with his evening meal. The explanation for the episode with Nina Ilyana did not lessen in any way the degradation he had felt. Instead the knowledge that they had been treating him as a sexual guinea pig sharpened his humiliation.

"If this is the price we have to pay for educating women," he retorted, "it would be better to leave them as they were. What could you ever understand except a male organ? And that of course you have never experienced."

Nina Ilyana acted as though this were exactly the reaction and the comment she had expected from him. She made notes industriously.

"Why not analyse yourself?" Hurford shouted. "To compensate for your unwanted body, you had to conceive intellectual pretensions."

Without a trace of smugness she replied: "I have been married twice and have four children."

237

"And your husbands? Were they able to copulate as often as you wanted?"

"It is not the number of times that matters, but the quality of the performance."

"Only in Russia would any man have taken you to his bed," Hurford ranted. "Peasants can't be choosers. In any civilised country you'd be put in charge of a lesbian brothel."

She ignored the insults and busied herself writing long notes. Watching her, Hurford was filled with remorse for his behaviour. The wretched woman was only doing what she believed was her duty.

After a time he told her: "I'm sorry. I should not have made that last remark."

"Don't ask my forgiveness, Michael." It was the first time she had used his Christian name. "Any offence against me is not important. But what has my country done to deserve your emnity?"

By the end of their session the pain

238

caused by two days and nights on the stool was unbearable. He began to believe and to hope that it could only be a question of hours before his strength succumbed. Unconsciousness beckoned him like a kindly doctor's prescription held out before a drug addict.

Lensky started the next bout of interrogation with his usual plea. "Don't you realise that you can't last out much longer? Why not tell us everything now? Then we'll know you acted through good motives and you'll be treated accordingly."

"And don't you realise I'll never tell you what you want? Before that my body will collapse. You'll learn nothing from an unconscious man."

"How wrong you are!" Lensky shook his head as though his prisoner's obtuseness pained him. "The system has been carefully devised to bring a collapse of the spirit before a physical breakdown. We know from experience that it always works."

For the first time Hurford realised exactly what kind of machine was being used against him. If the Russians had wished to force a confession from him through pain, they would have used other methods. The long hours of interrogation, lack of sleep, exhaustion and bodily discomfort were only ancillary to the main process, designed to reduce his resistance and leave him vulnerable to mental pressures.

He told himself that the Conveyor would not succeed with him, but anxiety was peeling away the outer layer of his self-confidence. The last session with Nina Ilyana had left him shaken and uneasy. They had reduced him from a man to a specimen and God only knew what the microscope would discover.

In the ablutions he tried to clean himself as well as he could, but the dirt accumulated after a week of squalor was beginning to be more and more apparent. He felt no satisfaction that the interrogation had been interrupted, only a growing sense of despondency. How could one man survive against the whole organisation of Soviet ruthlessness? If the Conveyor failed on him they would have other techniques, probably less humane, more degrading. There was nothing London could do for him now. He was alone.

Walking down the corridor to the cells they met another prisoner. He stood face to the wall, a watching guard beside him. Hurford could see nothing of the man except his prison suit, dark hair and a pair of grey, wasted hands pressed to the wall.

A sudden rage at the futility of the system gripped him. The urge to defy the regulations, to assert himself, was too strong to be controlled. Darting across the corridor, he elbowed the guard aside, seized the prisoner's shoulder and twisted him round.

"Are you another?" he demanded. "What sexual abberations have they discovered in your past?"

Quickly the two guards put an end

to his gesture. Hurford was pulled away before he had achieved anything. All he saw was abject fright in the other man's eyes.

As he was led to his cell he asked the guard: "Aren't you going to take me to the Prison Commissar? Won't I be put in the punishment cells?"

The man's reply was another humiliation. "Prisoners often behave like that at this stage."

Alone in his cell Hurford began to swear. With every filthy epithet he had ever heard, he railed on Russia, his interrogators, Savage, Nicole, Margery. The outburst relieved neither his anger nor his frustration. Instead as his rage spent itself, he found himself sobbing.

When eventually control returned, he had no appetite for the food which he had found waiting for him. He realised now that the Conveyor was doing its work. The non-stop interrogation with its changing themes, abuse, stripping away of privacy, appeals to his better nature, was driving him beyond the limits of endurance. Exposure to fluctuating and conflicting emotions of rage, remorse, shame, had stretched his nerves to a tension he had never before experienced. He could see the edge of a precipice but could only guess what lay beyond.

The real danger was that he might collapse and blurt out the truth without knowing or caring what he said. In a few minutes of instability everything could be destroyed. Using the remaining shreds of his concentration, he tried to work out what he must do. Somehow the Conveyor had to be stopped and an end put to the probing of the relentless machine.

Slowly his exhausted brain wound its way to the solution. A confession was the only thing that would satisfy the Russians, so they must be given one. To protect the truth, he must admit something.

When the guard came to fetch him, he immediately began to eat the meal on the tray. This gave him three or four extra minutes to work out a plan. One thing was clear. To halt the interrogation he would have to admit at least that he had been engaged in espionage. This did not seem to matter since they already had enough proof of that offence. They would also want to know what kind of information he had passed back to London and how it had been obtained. Here he must invent fictions plausible enough to satisfy the examiners. At all costs he must shelter any other person involved, Savage's precious source.

In the next session, while Krevana stormed and screamed his questions, Hurford developed his plan. By this time even thinking called for an immense effort. His mind was numbed by pain and the downpour that had been drumming on his emotions for more than sixty hours. At last he decided he was ready.

"Where did you obtain the photographs of classified Soviet documents that were found in your possession?"

"Can't you understand?" he shouted back at Krevana suddenly. "I know nothing of the photographs. They were planted by your stooges."

"Fornicator! Lying son of a bitch! You dare to accuse me?"

"Yes, I do," Hurford shouted. "What are you but a fat, ignorant peasant, a man who has made his way into a soft job by lying and bullying and sucking up to his superiors?"

"Pox-ridden capitalist! What are the names of your accomplices?"

Hurford struggled to his feet, hampered by his swollen muscles. "Stop your questions." He threatened Krevana with his fist. This display of histrionics, he found, was frighteningly easy. The passions he was simulating were not far below the surface. He shouted at the Russian: "I can't bear your voice any longer. Stop or I'll kill you."

It might have been imagination but he thought he detected a gleam of satisfaction behind Krevana's expression.

For a few moments he continued swearing and gesticulating.

Then he slumped back on to the stool and covered his face with his hands.

"I can't stand it!" he moaned. "I can't stand it!"

"Then all you need do is tell us what we wish to know."

"All right! All right! I'll tell you anything if only you'll leave me in peace."

He started to cry. The sobs could well have been real. Emotion was easy to squeeze out. Krevana waited patiently until it had subsided.

Then he said: "So! You're prepared to make a statement, are you?"

"Yes."

The Russian picked up the telephone. "Ask Examiner Lensky to come to room seven. Yes, it's urgent."

Lensky arrived looking as usual fresh and well-scrubbed. When Krevana told him that Hurford was ready to make a statement, his smile of pleasure was pretty with confusion, like a spinster who had just learnt that her vase arrangement had won first prize at the village show.

"I'm so glad you've made the right decision at last, Michael."

Krevana took a block of paper from the desk drawer and waited with his pen ready. His anger appeared to have been replaced by expectancy and satisfaction. The job was almost over.

"You are quite right," Hurford said in a low voice. "I have been working for British Intelligence."

"What was the name of the organisation that sent you here?"

He told them that and also that his immediate chief was Savage, which in any case they already knew. Of the rest of the set-up in London, he claimed ignorance, pointing out that this was his first assignment for them. To support his story, he sketched out not too accurately the way he had been recruited. There also seemed to be no point in denying that London had furnished him with the various pieces of flimsy equipment they had found in his apartment.

"Excellent, Michael!" Lensky exclaimed warmly. "You see how much better it is to be frank. And what a load off your conscience!"

Krevana demanded: "Now tell us the name of your contact in Moscow. Who has been feeding you the information?"

"I don't know who has been passing it. For all I know there may have been more than one person."

"Then how have you been operating? By dead-letter drops? In that case tell us where they were and when you used them."

"Not dead-letter drops," Hurford replied. He had suddenly remembered that there was a package still waiting in a cache, which he had been unable to collect. "Each time the information reached me by a different method following instructions sent to me by short-wave radio. The stuff you found on me, for example, came in a copy of *Pravda* which I bought from a paper stall in Manege Square."

"Describe the man who sold you it."

Hurford made up a plausible description for the fictitious newsvendor. Next, in answer to their questions, he explained how he had been passed secret material at other times, inventing on each occasion a method not too dissimilar to the actual operation he had carried out. To make sure that this real source could not be traced, he gave different dates and places. The photographs had been put in the pocket of his raincoat during a reception at the Peoples' Hall of Culture; instructions had been signalled to him by infra-red signal from a window in the Ministry of Foreign Trade; a microfilm of a document had been left in a chocolate bar wrapper on his seat at the State Circus.

"Excellent!" Lensky exclaimed as Krevana wrote out the statement laboriously in longhand. "And what kind of information was being passed to you?"

"I had no means of enlarging the microdots and finding out."

"And the photographs you found in your pocket?"

"They appeared to be plans of rocket launching sites."

Lensky glanced quickly at Krevana, as though this was a piece of news they had been expecting. By good fortune, Hurford felt, he had invented a detail which would add conviction to his story.

"How did you send your stuff back to London?"

There was no plausible lie, so he said: "Through a contact at the British Embassy."

"What was his name?"

"Pellew-Hawkes. He's the Press Attaché." Hurford had the name ready. He had already decided that if he must incriminate a member of the Embassy staff, it might as well be the Press Attaché whom he cordially disliked.

Lensky asked Hurford several more questions, mainly about details of the timing and location of his operations. These the K.G.B. would need if they planned to uncover his contacts. But Hurford felt confident he had contrived a lie elaborate enough to lead them nowhere.

When the full statement had been written out by Krevana, they gave it to Hurford to read. He worked his way through it slowly, insisting on small corrections in several places and Lensky appeared pleased with his thoroughness. Then they made him sign the statement and witnessed his signature with theirs.

"There, it was easier than you believed," Lensky, remarked amiably, gathering together the sheets of paper. "And now you deserve a rest."

Hurford shook him by the hand emotionally. "You have been my friend, Citizen Examiner. I'll never forget your kindness."

A guard led him back to his cell.

He collapsed on the bed, exhausted physically and mentally, wanting only sleep. But for a long time sleep would not come. Instead he started to wonder whether he had made the right decision in admitting even part of the truth. Might this not be exactly what the Russians wanted? Now perhaps they knew enough to uncover the rest. Doubt sprang from doubt, multiplying and burrowing insidiously through the sub-soil of his self-confidence. He knew now that he was unequipped to contend with the circumstances into which he had been thrust. Savage should have realised he was too old, too unadaptable, too vulnerable.

A piece of flotsam, he drifted at last to sleep on the tide of self-pity.

26

FOR two days he was left alone in his cell. Even the guards outside scarcely ever bothered to peer through the Judas window. He used the time to rest, conscious that he must recharge his physical resources and did nothing except lie on his bed. Meals and his morning and evening walks to the ablutions were the only interruptions to this routine.

To his surprise he found that although exhausted, he slept badly. The light in his cell which had scarcely bothered him during his first days in the Lubianka, was now a growing distraction. Nor could his mind rest. He found himself thinking always of the hours he spent on the Conveyor, going over every question he had been asked, trying to remember his exact answer. The fear that inadvertently he might have given something away obsessed him. Under the relentless barrage of questions, it would have been easy to make a slip, give the interrogators some tiny clue to the truth.

His sleep, when it came, was broken by dreams from which he awoke confused and trembling. Once in the diffuse softness between sleep and waking, he found himself shouting violent abuse; it was not the Russians that he was upbraiding but Savage.

After two days of idleness, instead of feeling rested, he was more exhausted. Physically he was in better shape, and the soreness and swelling around his thighs and groin had almost disappeared. But lack of sleep and hours of nagging worry prevented any real recuperation.

Soon another idea appeared to harass him. If the K.G.B. discovered that his confession was on all germane points a fabrication, he would be put back on the Conveyor. Hurford was certain that he would never be able to endure another ordeal like the last. He would collapse, give in, tell them everything. Before long the prospect terrified him.

On the morning of the third day, when he felt helpless with anxiety about the future and his own condition, the prison doctor visited him unexpectedly. He realised that this was another of those gifts of fortune, providence coming to the rescue of the weak.

"How are you keeping, Citizen?" the doctor asked. He was a man whose almost excessive cheerfulness did not disguise an absolute professionalism. All the time Hurford felt his eyes, probing, dispassionate, analytical, examining his patient.

"To tell the truth, I'm sleeping badly."

"That's not surprising. This isn't exactly a convalescent home. Anything else?"

"My nerves are a bit shaky. And really that's unusual for me. I can't remember when I was last unwell."

"I'm sure that's true. A healthy, well-balanced man. It's probably nothing to worry about, but I'll look you over just to make certain."

He gave Hurford a swift, professional examination. As he worked, he talked cheerfully and informally, building up a relationship that was as relaxing as it was reassuring. Hurford could only admire the man. If the National Health Service at home was staffed with doctors as capable as this, Harley Street would soon be depopulated.

"There's nothing organically wrong with you," the doctor said, when he had finished. "But you need a tonic."

"A tonic?" Hurford felt disillusioned. "The mixture as before?"

The Russian smiled. "No. Not a patent medicine. We don't use them in the Soviet. I'll put you on a mild stimulant for a few days."

"Wouldn't a sedative be more effective?"

"Not in your case. You need something to sharpen your appetite, raise your spirits. That would end your sleeping problems."

From the white medical bag he was carrying, he took a box of capsules and gave one to Hurford. It was yellow, translucent and about half an inch long. Hurford swallowed it with the dregs of tea that remained in his mug from the morning meal. The doctor left, promising to visit him again the next day.

By afternoon the stimulant must have taken effect for Hurford felt distinctly better. Most of his depression had dissipated and the fears that had been torturing his mind no longer seemed so alarming. The answers he had given Krevana and the others were watertight, he felt certain. In any case Savage and his bunch in London were well able to look after themselves.

In the early morning he felt lively enough to take exercise, pacing up and down the cell and trying out a few elementary gymnastics. After the evening meal he tried to exercise his brain as well, first by reciting poetry. At the age of fourteen he had once learnt the whole of Browning's *Rabbi Ben Ezra* to please an English teacher whom he admired. Though he had never repeated even a stanza of the poem since, he found now to his astonishment that he could remember every line.

Tiring of poetry he began to play an imaginary game of chess. This was an exercise in concentration and visual memory that he had often attempted when imprisoned by the Germans during the war, with scant success. Today he contrived a long and complex game, remembering every move, till Black checkmated White on the fifty-second.

That night he slept well, but by morning the lethargy had returned, accompanied by a depression that was if anything more acute. He was relieved when the doctor arrived and gave him another capsule. The treatment was continued on the days following and apart from the short spells of almost suicidal despondency which recurred each morning, Hurford was certain that his condition was improving.

On the afternoon of the sixth day after his release from the Conveyor, a guard came into the cell and took him to an interrogation room. He decided immediately that the K.G.B. had exposed his confession as a sham and that Krevana and his colleagues would be put to work again to crush his resistance. The prospect did not alarm him as much as he had expected. Looking back, he suspected that the strain and irritation and physical discomfort had not been as severe as they had seemed at the time. Now that he knew the form, he was better equipped to handle the tricks of the examiners and would put up a better show.

To his surprise, it was the Assistant Prosecutor who was waiting in room seven. His manner was affable.

"How are they treating you, Mr.

Hurford? Are you well?"

"Very fit, considering the conditions in this prison. And ready for any interrogation you can devise."

"There's no question of that. There are just one or two small points in your statement which I would be grateful if you would clarify."

Hurford felt almost cheated, as though he had been deprived of the chance of proving himself. The Prosecutor continued: "First there is the matter of your visit to the State Circus, on the occasion when information was passed to you. In your statement you said that you thought this was on a Tuesday. I wonder whether you could try and fix the date more precisely."

Other similar questions followed, most of them concerned with minor details of fact in his confession. The interview lasted only for about forty minutes, after which he was allowed to return to his cell.

That night his sleep was interrupted in a bizarre manner. He had been sleeping deeply for what must have been several hours when he was woken by a violent noise. It was so loud that several seconds passed before he realised it was music. The sound came sweeping into the confined space of the cell, bouncing back off the walls, shattering the silence.

His senses stunned, Hurford could not understand what had happened It was pop music; records of British and American groups which he could remember hearing when Nicole had her transistor switched on, which was most of the working day. At first, in spite of its monstrously loud volume, the music did not disturb him. In a way it was a contact with the outside world which, he realised now, he badly needed. But after several minutes the unvarying raucousness, the rhythmic monotony, began to get on his nerves. He had given the K.G.B. what they wanted and was entitled to sleep.

The music continued for perhaps half an hour. Vainly he tried to deaden it by wrapping his blanket round his head. Finally growing desperate, he got up, crossed to the cell door and began beating on it and shouting to attract the attention of the guards.

Before anybody heard or took notice, the music stopped abruptly. He returned to bed but for a long time could not sleep. The strident tunes, with their simple, repetitive harmonies, still seemed to be swirling round the room. Hurford's indignation also lingered, diminishing to petulance only gradually.

Next morning when the doctor came he complained to him. "How can any treatment you give me be expected to work when I am kept awake half the night by music?"

"Music? You must be mistaken."

"God, I wish I was! It nearly drove me crazy."

"What kind of music?"

"Pop. The usual frenetic screaming of the beat groups."

The doctor looked at him searchingly.

"Come now, think again! Could it not have been a nightmare?"

"You don't believe me? It kept me awake for hours. I even got out of bed and tried to call the guards."

"I'm afraid it isn't possible. There is no equipment for relaying music into the cells."

Hurford wondered whether this was an elaborate hoax or possibly an off-beat way of testing his mental and physical condition. He said: "You'll never convince me. I know bloody well it was music that kept me awake. And it was unbearably loud, ridiculously so."

"Wait a moment."

The doctor went and knocked on the door of the cell which was opened immediately by a guard who must have been standing ready outside. He spoke to the guard rapidly and quietly and then beckoned to Hurford.

"Come with me." They went into the hall outside. "There is one way to show you that you were mistaken."

The guard opened the door to the cell next to Hurford's own. Inside an old man in a prison suit sat hunched on the bed. He looked up anxiously when they went in. The doctor pointed to the old man and told Hurford: "Ask him about the music. If it was as loud as you claim, he must have heard it too."

"What is it? What do you want?" the man demanded plaintively. His Russian carried a heavy, coarse accent that Hurford could not identify. The structure of his face and head was Asiatic.

"Did you hear music in the middle of the night?"

"What music?"

"Western records. Teen-age music. Surely it woke you?"

"I heard no music."

"You must have done!" Hurford insisted. "It was loud enough to have roused the whole prison."

"I heard nothing."

They went outside. While the guard

264

was locking the door of the cell, Hurford said to the doctor: "That man is plainly terrified. He only said what he thought you wanted him to say."

"Then try the cell on the other side of yours. This time I'll stay outside."

The occupant of the other cell was a younger man with closely cropped hair and a scarred face. He was pacing up and down talking to himself when the guard opened the door. Hurford introduced himself.

"I'm the prisoner from the cell next to this. I need your help."

"You must be someone important, if they allow you to speak to other prisoners." From his voice and bearing, he was an educated man, a scientist or an engineer perhaps. There was a trace of amused tolerance in his attitude to Hurford.

"Last night I was woken by deafeningly loud music."

"Really?"

"When I complained to the authorities, they denied that there was any music.

They're trying to make out I imagined it."

"How can I help?"

"You must have heard the racket as well. I want you to confirm what I told them."

"Sorry. I'd like to but I can't."

"There's nothing to be afraid of. You won't be victimised."

The man's smile was almost patronising. "That wouldn't worry me. But I'm afraid I heard nothing."

Back in Hurford's cell, the doctor asked him: "Well, are you satisfied?"

"Certainly not! I know bloody well I heard music. This is some sort of trick."

The doctor did not argue. "In addition to your usual medicine, I'll give you a mild sedative which you can take at night. That will make sure your sleep is undisturbed."

Alone, Hurford looked suspiciously at the single pink pill in its tiny box. No one would ever convince him that the music which had shattered his night had been just a dream or an illusion. It had been too loud, too well defined and had lasted too long. Even now he could hear the words of the songs and feel the energy of the rhythm.

He tried to forget about the matter, but the idea kept returning. If this was a plot or trick, what was the point of it? If not, how could he prove to the doctor that what he had heard was not a fantasy?

Late in the evening he decided not to take the pill. Instead he crushed it with his heel and swept the powdered fragments into the cracks and corners of the stone floor.

That night he was awakened three times. The music was the same as the previous night. It came swirling into the cell, assaulting his senses, battering down thought. Each session was shorter, lasting for not more than ten minutes, but long enough to wake him thoroughly and revive his indignation.

When it started for the third time,

he got out of bed angrily. There must be somewhere in the cell a concealed loudspeaker or grill through which the sound emerged. He would find it, show it to the doctor next morning and prove his point. Carefully he searched every part of the cell; the stonework around the door and window, the floor under the bed, the ceiling behind the light bulb He found nothing.

Next morning he told the doctor, raising his voice: "This has got to stop! Three times that infernal music woke me last night."

"In spite of the sedative?"

"I didn't take your blasted pill."

"That was very unwise. It's most important that you get plenty of sleep."

"Then tell that to the Prison Commissar. Get the music stopped."

"You really must accept what I say. There is no music."

"Are you saying that I'm going mad?" Hurford shouted truculently.

The doctor did not reply at once. Like a man with unpleasant news, he looked at Hurford, wondering how much he should be told.

"Not at all. You're simply suffering from severe mental stress. The condition is not uncommon. Plenty of prisoners show the same symptoms as you; depression, irritability and a tendency to mild hallucinations. Some doctors call it prison melancholia."

After giving him the daily stimulant, the doctor went away leaving another pink pill behind. "Now take this without fail," he said as he handed it over in its box.

Hurford placed the box under the blanket on his bed. He did not want to look at it. The Russians, he knew now, were engineering a plot against him and the pill was part of it. So were the prisoners who occupied the two cells on either side of his own. An old frightened man and an arrogant intellectual; what did they have in common? He tried to puzzle it out, to see how the pieces of the plot might interlock.

By this time the K.G.B. must have discovered that a substantial part of his statement was false. Since he had not been submitted to the Conveyor once more, the authorities were clearly relying on another way of extracting from him what they wished to know. It must be a new and elaborate method that did not require cross-examination. So they must be expecting him to betray himself.

"It's all very well for the patriots back home," he said aloud, "but I'm alone, facing the whole of the K.G.B. And in spite of all his assurances, Savage won't be much help to me here."

Could Savage be involved in the plot as well, he wondered. It was not past possibility that he might be working as a double agent. The idea he realised was ridiculous but it kept returning to plague him.

In the afternoon he was taken to the interrogation room for more inoffensive questioning. This time it was Lensky who interviewed him. He went over Hurford's statement like a conscientious solicitor checking the first draft of a contract with his client. His manner and the futility of the questions he posed, angered Hurford but he controlled his temper. On no account must he let the Russians suspect that he knew this was all a façade to hide the deeper stratagem they were employing against him.

Back in his cell, he peeped under the blanket. The pill box was still there. He folded the blanket twice so that there would be four thicknesses to cover it. There was no need to look inside the box. He knew the pill was there because he could feel it watching him.

"My God!" he exclaimed. "That's it!"

Music was being beamed into his cell from an invisible source. With the same technique, a sophisticated refinement of electronics, they were keeping a watch on him, trying to read his thoughts and so wring an involuntary confession from him. A nation so advanced in science might easily have developed a device that could receive impulses from the human brain, translate them into signals, feed them into a kind of decoding machine. And the theory fitted the facts. This explained the long hours he had been left alone in his cell, the patience of the interrogators, the attentiveness of the doctor. The doctor must be the clue to the whole affair because why else had he come to visit Hurford? The Russians were not renowned for caring about their prisoners' well-being.

The answer came in a flash of inspiration. The so-called stimulant they had been giving him was a form of tracer which made his mental processes more perceptible to their scanning device. And the pink pill of course was the bugging device, a masterpiece of miniaturisation, developed no doubt for space research.

The brilliance of his discovery

astounded him. By analytic deduction he had arrived at the truth in time to save himself and the whole operation Savage had planned. Had he swallowed the pill, the game would have been up, the secrets revealed.

Now he must get rid of the pill. To destroy it would not be enough. It must continue to send back its signals to the coding machine, even if it had nothing to report. Then the machine would record nothing, no thought patterns, an empty brain. He chuckled at the idea. The watching Russians would take him for an imbecile or innocent.

Carefully, as he had seen bomb disposal men work, he took the pill from its box. By standing on the chair, he could just reach the single window in the cell. Pushing thumb and forefinger through the bars, he dropped the deadly device into the outside world.

27

THAT night he lay awake, his brain as sharp as a freshly cut diamond, waiting for the music. On no account must he allow it to come in and catch him unprepared. The melodies could easily be beamed in on a two-way wave which would suck the secrets from his mind and carry them back to the control room. He could almost see the K.G.B. technicians sitting at their instruments, waiting for the first signals.

After several hours, when no music had come, he knew he was defeating them. This was the answer to their scheme. By staying awake, he could jam their electronic contraption with the powerful beam of his conscious mind. Early morning came and a haggard light filtered into the cell, so he knew he was safe. Exhausted, but satisfied, he let himself sink back into the suffocating warmth of sleep.

For two more days the struggle continued as he thwarted all the efforts of the K.G.B. to destroy his silence with science. On the third morning he woke suddenly, to find Savage's eye staring at him through the Judas window in the door. Almost immediately it disappeared. Jumping from his bed, he ran to the door and thumped on it.

"Bernard," he called urgently. "I'm in here."

A key turned and the door opened. Outside stood the figure of a uniformed guard. "What do you want?"

He turned and went back to his bed. The voice was not the voice of Savage, nor was the face, but Hurford knew it was him. With a new form of instant disguise, Savage was able to fool the Russians. Just in time Hurford realised that he must say or do nothing that would give Savage away. He heard the door being locked again.

Excitement prevented him from sleeping again. He had been wrong to doubt London for they had not abandoned him. This was the first move in a plan to rescue him. At any moment there would be action and he must be prepared, reflexes alerted. When a guard brought his morning meal, he searched the food for a hidden message and, finding none, gulped it down quickly.

The next two days he spent in high-pitched expectancy. Three more times Savage's eye appeared at the spyhole in the door. Aware that he must make no move that would wreck the plan, Hurford gave no sign that he even recognised him.

The prison doctor came in daily, gave him the stimulant capsule which he swallowed obediently and the treacherous sedative which he later dropped through the window bars. It could only be while he slept that the Russians could destroy him. So he slept during the day to outwit them, but only in brief snatches.

After a few days he noticed that his body was growing curiously light, until it seemed to float a few inches above the bed.

Time also ceased to function and a moment of rest extended towards infinity. He neither knew nor cared how long this phase of his imprisonment lasted. Days and nights, weeks and months meant nothing, all he must do was wait.

Sometimes he thought of Nicole. It would not be long before he was with her again and the prospect filled him with a lust more exciting than anything he had ever known. The things he would do to her! He knew now that he could rise above physical limitations, transcend her passion with an inexhaustible vitality which would burn like a crimson flame and consume them both. The idea excited him so much that it exhausted him, leaving him trembling.

The Russians must have realised that he was defeating them, because they redoubled their efforts to break his control. They tried another trick, which was to dim the light in his cell gradually to a faint red glow. Then when his eyes had grown accustomed to it, they switched back to a light of dazzling intensity, so bright that it hurt his eyes. He only laughed. The childish simpletons did not realise that the light was helping to keep him awake and so outwit the electronic thought-reading machine.

Quite by chance he also discovered that the floor of his cell was live with electricity. It was only a low voltage, enough to make his feet tingle and no more, but he knew that it had a sinister purpose. So he kept his feet off the ground as much as possible and took exercise by walking backwards and forwards on top of his bed.

Then one afternoon, he had no means of knowing the date, he was taken out for exercise. For twenty minutes they allowed him to walk round a small grimy area at the back of the prison. The combined effects of daylight, fresh air and the effort of walking soon tired him, so he rested, leaning against the wall and watching the sky, in case a helicopter might swoop down to whisk him away. That was the kind of rescue that Savage's schoolboy imagination would contrive and enjoy.

No helicopter came. On the way back to the cells, the guard took him to a wash room that he had not visited before. It differed from the ablutions which he normally used, in that it had a mirror fixed to the wall above the washbasins.

He stared at his reflection and was paralysed with surprise. Cadaverous eyes stared back at him out of a thin face, framed with unkempt hair and a rough beard. The face, as one would have expected, was only a mask, but what shocked him was to see that the eyes were not his but Savage's.

Mocking, sardonic, they went with him as he followed the guard back to his cell. Crossing the floor in two great leaps to limit his exposure to the alien rays, he climbed on to the bed and sat there, trying to grasp the implications of his discovery.

Savage had moved into the Lubianka with him, sharing not just his imprisonment, but his body. What did it mean?

The bloody fool has blundered, he thought, been too clever by half, this is not going to rescue anyone, instead we're both in here, on our own and helpless.

After several hours suspicion began to seep into his mind, welling up through the chinks in his composure. He remembered his earlier speculation that Savage might be working for the Russians. And with doubt came terror.

They were going to liquidate him. Savage's mind was entering his body, forcing out his own, pushing him into the vast black void outside. The devilish cleverness of the plot made him gasp.

One push and the being that was Hurford would go spiralling down into infinity, leaving no trace. London wished to eliminate him because he had failed.

He sprang up, his fear of the electrified floor obliterated by this new danger. Where was the weapon he needed to save him? Where was the shining sword of the angel? Every muscle in his body was afflicted by a violent palsy and he could not stop shaking.

"Get out, Savage!" he yelled as loudly as his quivering throat would allow. "Leave my body, damn you!"

The cunning devil could only have entered his body through his mouth. Opening it he thrust his fingers in to seize the intruder. The effort made him retch and he cried out again, screaming: "Get thee hence!"

For minutes he struggled, writhing and screaming. High-pitched profanities echoed round the four walls of the cell. Then, suddenly, the paroxysm stopped, his whole body stiffened. For an instant he stood rigid, staring ahead and then slumped to the ground.

He was in a coma for eight hours. When consciousness returned, he remembered nothing of the hallucinations. A guard led him to interrogation room number seven where Lensky was waiting.

"Don't you think the time has come, Michael, to settle accounts?"

"I suppose so."

"It's not too late to undo the wrong you have done our country."

Hurford listened while the Russian talked, elaborating on the theme of his guilt and how he could make amends. The man was so persuasive, so friendly, that he was moved by remorse and wanted to weep. One could not argue against such simple logic. Nor did he wish to. He knew that he had held different opinions but now they seemed utterly remote, ideas from another age. His mind had been reborn, free of prejudice, empty of everything.

"Do you recognise that you did wrong?"

"Yes, Citizen Examiner," Hurford said sincerely. His evil behaviour of the past loomed black and disgraceful. "And I'll do whatever you suggest."

Part Three

Development

28

BRITISH CONSUL TO SEE HURFORD

RUSSIANS RELENT

From our correspondent — Moscow, November 7th

"THE British Consul is to see Michael Hurford in the Lubianka Prison tomorrow. The news was given by the Press Attaché from the British Embassy early this morning; so early that the Press Attaché was still wearing his bedroom slippers as he entertained us to coffee and caviar in a room of ornate nineteenth-century splendour. A lecturer at the British Institute here, Hurford has been detained in Moscow's famous prison for more than two months and until now the Soviet authorities have steadfastly refused to allow Embassy officials to see him. Nor have any charges against him been announced.

"Today's news leads one to believe that Hurford has now been officially charged and will soon be put on trial. There is also general agreement in informed circles that he has probably confessed to the offences of which he has been accused. In this case a public trial seems certain and will probably not be long postponed.

"Interest in Hurford's case will be particularly high, following the recent trial and conviction in Britain of the Russian agent, Donaldson. Only four weeks ago Donaldson, a Russian spy who posed as an American businessman, was sentenced to fifteen years imprisonment at the Old Bailey, after being found guilty of offences against the Official Secrets Act.

"It seems likely that the Embassy in Moscow will now seek permission for Mrs. Margery Hurford to visit her husband in prison. Mrs. Hurford, whose home is in Camberley, has told the Foreign Office that she is ready to fly to Russia at a moment's notice if permission can be arranged."

29

"DON'T think me impertinent, Margery, but an old friend can ask these questions. Are you sure Mike will want to see you?"

Savage was lunching with Margery Hurford at the Vendôme. His telephone call had surprised her, but when he had hinted that he wished to talk about her impending trip to Moscow, she had come up from Camberley by train. He had also told her that her rail fare, first class, would be paid. In a way, Margery thought, it was just like the old days.

"Oh, Bernard, of course he will! After all these months locked up in that ghastly place? He'll forget about the past. Besides, there's no one else who can go. His mother is dead and his father's too old. Can't you see? I feel I have to show the world that I'll stick by him."

"I quite understand. In any case, it's your decision."

"I wonder whether I should take him anything? Clothes perhaps, or cigarettes."

"He doesn't smoke. And the Embassy will advise you on what you'll be allowed to take in."

Savage could not recall when he had last seen Margery. In a few years she had changed perceptibly. Her face, once a composition of delicate features, had coarsened and the arched nose had a predatory look, the mouth was slack and dissipated.

"My real object in seeing you was to warn you, Margery, that you must expect to find Mike very changed."

"In what way?"

"He must have been through quite an ordeal. The Russians don't spare their prisoners."

Margery's blue eyes, faded now below wrinkled lids, opened wide. It was a trick of hers, he remembered. "Do you mean torture?"

"No. Worse than that, brain-washing."

"Mike won't tell them anything. You know how brave he was in the war when he was in the bag. Of course he's dreadfully stubborn and perhaps that's the same thing."

"Now listen, Margery, you must accept this," Savage told her firmly. "By now he will have told them everything. Otherwise you wouldn't be going to Moscow."

"Mike a traitor? That's impossible!"

"I wish you'd understand that it's not a question of treachery, or of failure through cowardice. The Russians use techniques that eventually break the resistance of any man, however brave he may be. In fact, the only people who would not be affected by brain-washing would be subnormal, morons. With the healthy, intelligent man, it's only a question of time."

Margery shuddered delicately. "What are these techniques?"

"Psychological. They work on their prisoners scientifically, playing on human weaknesses. First they humiliate and degrade them, then expose them to long periods of fear and anxiety. It's more subtle than it sounds. The interrogation is prolonged and varied, inducing first anger, then guilt, then despair."

"If it's only interrogation it can't be so dreadful."

"The human brain is not as robust as you imagine. If it is subjected to a stress acute enough and prolonged enough, it must finally give way. The Russians induce the stress by endless interrogation and then, if necessary, speed up the process with drugs."

"They've been drugging him?" This was something that Margery could accept. She had a belief in the power of chemical substances that was almost superstition.

"Eventually the stress gets too great for the prisoner's mind to support and it collapses. The subject has what is virtually a nervous breakdown."

"Poor Mike!"

"They call it transmarginal inhibition.

293

It's a kind of protective mechanism which the brain employs as a last resort when it has been pushed beyond endurance. The victim goes into a coma. When he recovers it is as though his mind had been wiped clean. His normal judgement and critical faculties have been impaired. Usually he accepts without question whatever suggestions are made to him. That is how the Russians get their confessions. In the end the prisoner admits whatever they want him to, quite willingly. Often he can be converted to their ideas."

"How horrible!"

"Yes. And of course all this has a pretty drastic effect on a man. It's no exaggeration to say that he finishes up as a nervous wreck. Recovery is a slow process. You mustn't expect to find Mike looking well or behaving normally."

They finished their lunch, talking not about Hurford but about the Army. Living in Camberley, Margery had managed to keep in touch with the movements of almost everyone they had known in the old days. Nostalgic gossip was almost her only pleasure now and one of her few talents.

Over coffee and Benedictine she said sweetly: "Thank you so much, Bernard dear. I can't remember when I last had such a lovely time."

"Now you go easy on that husband of yours," he lectured her, smiling, as he put her in a taxi for Waterloo.

30

"YOU look better than I thought you would, Mike."

"I feel fine," Hurford lied. He was filled with an overwhelming sense of depression which never seemed to lift except when the prison doctor gave him a stimulant. The doctor's visits were less frequent now.

"One hears so many stories about how they treat their prisoners."

"I can't complain. On the contrary they've been more than fair to me."

Depression apart, it was true he felt better, if only because the Russians had allowed him to wear his own clothes again. His suit, expertly repaired, had been returned to him and with it a pair of new shoes. A barber had cut his hair and was shaving him daily, because the authorities still would not trust him with a razor. All these changes dated back to the day when the British Consul had been given permission to visit him.

"I thought you'd look terrible; straight from Belsen. But you're a bit thin, nothing more." Margery felt she had to repeat her assurances, because when she had entered the room she had scarcely recognised the man with the sunken eyes and grey skin.

"No, they've treated me well."

Before he met Margery, Hurford had been warned by the Prison Commissar that if he said anything against the Soviet Union, the meeting would be immediately stopped. The warning was unnecessary for he did not feel at all disposed to slander Russia or the Russians. The only bitterness that he felt was against London.

"You're really in the headlines back home," Margery said. "Quite famous."

"Infamous, I should think." He smiled back but was thinking that this was the reason she had come, to share a little of his synthetic fame, to be photographed for the papers, to be interviewed for television when she got home.

She put her hand on his and squeezed it. "Don't worry, Mike, everybody is with you. The papers have all denounced the Russians for the way they've treated you."

"What do you mean?"

"Keeping you locked up all these months and not allowing the Ambassador to even see you."

"Months?" Hurford frowned, trying to remember what he had been doing for the past few months. Surely it had only been days since he was brought to the Lubianka?

"When you get back there'll be a hero's welcome waiting for you. Mark my words."

"Get back? I don't think I'll ever return to England."

"But, Mike, they can't possibly convict you!"

"Don't be ridiculous, Margery, of course they will. The trial will be only a formality. The Russians know I was working for Bernard Savage's crowd."

That could only mean, she realised, that he had confessed. She was going to ask him reproachfully why, but then she remembered what Savage had told her. Instead she asked cautiously: "What do you think will happen?"

"They could shoot me, but I don't think they will. With any luck I'll get a lenient sentence. Perhaps only ten years."

"Ten years!" Margery was appalled. The exciting dreams she had constructed, a romantic reconciliation, a new life, an end to her loneliness, crumpled and fell like a set for an epic film.

"It could be reduced for good behaviour. In any case, after I've served my sentence, I may stay here if they'll let me."

"In Russia? You can't be serious!"

"I've never been more serious in my life."

"But what would you do here? Teach?" She stared at him and saw a mask that was only partly familiar, through which an alien spirit uttered words she could not comprehend.

Savage had been right after all. Mike was a little round the bend.

"There's so much to do in Russia and through Russia in Europe. A whole new society to build."

His voice was colourless, his expression flat. His new visions did not appear to have fired his enthusiasm. Margery changed the subject. She felt ill-at-ease, like on the occasion when at the age of fourteen she had been taken to the bedside of her dying mother. The woman she had seen then, with face deformed through pain, had been a stranger whose feeble gaze made Margery want to shrink away.

"Bernard gave me a lovely lunch," she said brightly and thinking that the tale could do with improvement added: "At the Savoy."

Hurford looked at her with quick suspicion. "Did Bernard arrange your visit here?"

"Oh, no. The F.O. asked me if I would like to come." She lied again because it was she who had approached the Foreign Office.

"Then why did Bernard want to see you?"

"He's very worried about you. He asked me to tell you that they'll do all they can."

His hand rested on the table in front of him. She noticed that it trembled as he said slowly: "You can tell that bastard to go to hell!"

31

S AVAGE met Colonel Fenton by
the bear pit in the Zoo. The
bear pit was a good place to
talk. Scarcely anyone went to look at
the mangy beasts that wandered up
and down outside their artificial caves,
staring moodily across the trench which
protected them from the grimy humans
that waited menacingly beyond. Savage
felt that it was totally unnecessary and
more than a little theatrical to arrange
meetings at the Zoo. It was the sort
of thing the *Daily Express* would go
mad about, if the story ever leaked
out. On the other hand, he knew
privately that every Thursday Fenton
had a golf lesson with Percy Holdright
a hundred yards away. By arranging a
meeting at the Zoo, the colonel could
justify charging up the return taxi fare
to Regent's Park. The colonel had nice

scruples in money matters.

"Hurford's trial starts tomorrow."

"There's nothing we can do," Savage replied, "except keep our legs crossed."

"The press isn't letting up on us at all. Did you see today's leader in *The Times*?"

"You mustn't take *The Times* seriously. It dates you. People only read the leaders to count the clichés. *The Times* is strictly light reading now; the intellectual's comic strip."

Fenton was not easily tranquillised. He said: "More questions tabled in the House today."

Savage laughed and threw a bun towards the bears. "You should have some sympathy for our needier members. They have to justify the pocket-money that the unions pay them."

They strolled away from the bears, past the sea-lions towards the penguins. Around them animal life chattered on, suitably muted for human eardrums; endless fornication, a little incest and nothing more than the merest trace of cannibalism.

Outside the monkey cage Fenton stopped and said morosely: "The do-gooders are all lined up against us, their muskets primed with powder from the Kremlin. I wonder if we could divert some of their fire."

"Towards our transatlantic cousins?" Savage knew at once what he was suggesting. Such was the rapport between them.

"I don't see why we should carry all the odium of inefficiency, particularly when it's not deserved."

Together they watched the surprising sexual performance of two chimpanzees. Savage remembered with nostalgia a little Armenian girl who had been introduced to him by his batman in Tel Aviv.

"From the stuff we've had back from Moscow so far," Savage said, "Research have compiled a list of two hundred and thirty-six Soviet agents of one type or another now in the States."

"What fun to pass over the lot! Think of the row and the heads that would fall! But we can't do that even to the Yanks. Pick out a dozen and send Washington their names and all we know about them. Then we can leak a suitable story to the Press. British Intelligence exposes weaknesses in American security. You know the kind of thing."

"That line won't be easy to put over."

"You must have a friend in Fleet Street."

"Heaven forbid! But I have two enemies who hate each other which is just as good."

Fenton looked at his watch. He was meeting his wife's cousin, a recently elected Member of Parliament for a Bristol constituency, in the Carlton Club at twelve-thirty. Savage read the signal and began walking a little faster past the monkeys.

"What about Hurford?" Fenton asked.

"From what his wife says there isn't

much doubt that the Russians have broken him down. He was pretty vindictive about us, I gather."

"The Russians must be very sure of themselves. I hear that part of the trial is even to be televised."

The monkeys chattered at them mockingly as they passed. One reached out through the bars and tried to grab Fenton's bowler. He rapped its paw severely with his umbrella.

"Have you ever noticed," Savage observed, "that in relation to the size of its body, a monkey's organ is pitifully small?"

"That is one of the boons that God granted us to single us out from the beasts. It behoves us to make the best possible use of it."

"Darwin would see the flaw in your argument," Savage replied. "But I'm damned if I can."

32

THE spectators in the Great Hall of the Soviet Supreme Court muttered angrily as the prisoner was brought in. Of the several hundred that had been admitted almost half were demonstrators, detailed by local party organisations, whose duty would be to applaud the performance of the Prosecutor and show anger as the villainous crimes of the accused were unfolded. The rest were conscientious citizens, all Communist Party members because tickets were not available to anyone outside the Party, who had come to see the British spy get his deserts.

"Although you will feel horror and revulsion as the vile crimes of the accused are exposed," the Prosecutor opened by saying, "the case is extremely simple. By his own confession Hurford was recruited by British Intelligence and sent here under the false guise of a lecturer at the British Institute, thus abusing the hospitality of the peace-loving Soviet Union, which had encouraged the creation of the Institute in the vain hope of furthering better relations with the West."

The crowd murmured disapprovingly. Seated in the prisoners' pen, a microphone in front of him, a uniformed soldier behind, Hurford knew that the trial was only a spectacle, painstakingly contrived and rehearsed to create the greatest possible effect. Russian might must be underlined, Russian virtue upheld.

He felt no resentment. The only thought that worried him was the fear that he would break down in court. In the past few days he had felt his whole personality crushed in a fearful melancholy. Unreasonable fears plucked at nerves which were already taut and guilt, remorse and hopelessness engulfed him, driving out all other thoughts. More than once as he sat in his cell, he had found tears running down his cheeks.

Across the hall in the most distant part of the court, the journalists from the West were clustered. He had seen the scanning dials of their faces swivel towards him when he entered and then tilt down again as pencils moved towards notebooks.

"You will hear how, when the prisoner was arrested, various articles were found in his apartment which could only have been intended for use in espionage."

Hurford's radio, camera and binoculars were produced in court. The Prosecutor held them up in turn, described their functions and sent them to be put before the five judges on their rostrum. Three of the judges were high-ranking army officers who wore their uniforms. The other two were women, one also in uniform and the other a civilian in a blue costume. All five watched the proceedings with nothing more than analytical interest. To Hurford it seemed that this impassivity invested them with a far more impressive and frightening majesty than any wig or ermine.

"Also in possession of the accused was found a far more damaging piece of evidence. He was carrying a letter addressed to England which he subsequently admitted he was going to post through diplomatic channels. The letter was examined and fixed on it were a number of microdots which, when enlarged, turned out to be copies of documents of the highest strategic importance to the Soviet Union. For reasons of security I am unable to reveal the exact nature of these documents but they will be shown to the Judge President and his colleagues later, when the public and the press have been excluded from this court."

This was the first time Hurford had heard that any part of the trial was to be held in camera. He was surprised. From what he could remember, none of the information he had passed back to London had seemed to possess military significance.

"In the meantime we have the confession of the accused that he collected information prejudicial to the security of the Soviet and passed it back to his chiefs in London. I feel I am bound to add that in every case this information was relayed to London with the assistance of personnel from the British Diplomatic Mission in Moscow. This proves yet again how the corrupt capitalist governments of the West are prepared to misuse in a disgraceful manner the courtesies and conventions of diplomacy between civilised nations."

From the benches of the spectators came a muted rumble of rage. The Western journalists lifted their pencils from their notebooks and grinned cynically at each other, apart from one Italian who took it all down verbatim for eleven million Communists.

"Finally," the Prosecutor was saying,

"you will be shown how the prisoner himself described to us a place where he was to find certain documents which he would then pass on to his contact. Officials of the Security Police went to this place and they will tell you of the material they found there. This material is evidence of a most damning nature that incriminates beyond any shadow of doubt the Soviet national, I will not honour her with the name of citizen, who was so weak and so easily corrupted as to betray her country by helping this man."

For almost the first time since his arrest and imprisonment, Hurford was stirred by curiosity. Because of the intensive security precautions that London had built into his method of operation, he had not the slightest idea of who his contact might be. After he had made his final confession the K.G.B. had questioned him again and again on every detail of his operations. Twice he had been made to look through sheaves of identity photographs but had found no likeness that he recognised On another occasion, only a few days before the trial, he had been asked to look through the spy-hole of a cell at a grey-haired man inside. At first he thought he had never seen the man before but, after further talks with the examiners, he had begun to wonder whether the face was not after all familiar. Lensky had told him that he must have seen the man on his visit to the Bolshoi theatre and after thinking about this, he was certain that Lensky was right. Even so he did not know the man's name.

Now it appeared that his contact was not a man after all, but a woman. She must be the precious source which Savage had mentioned; the source London wanted so desperately to exploit. To learn that the source had now been uncovered and stopped up, did not cause Hurford the slightest concern.

"At this stage I propose to have this wretched collaborator brought into court and she will stand trial with the prisoner."

A door at one side of the hall opened and with a well-timed touch of drama, a woman was brought in by two female guards. She was about thirty-five and looked, as she walked slowly past the front row of spectators and court officials, frighteningly fragile. In the normal way her face would not have been unattractive but now there was nothing but indifference and pallor, two dead pine cones fallen in soiled snow.

Hurford glanced at her curiously as she was led into the prisoners' pen and made to sit down at the far end. He could not recall ever seeing her before, but the events of the past few weeks had taught him not to trust his memory.

"This woman is Valentina Vanovitch," the Prosecutor announced. "Until recently she held a responsible position as personal assistant to the Director General of one of our most important government departments, a position which she shamelessly betrayed. By her own admission she was guilty of copying documents of the greatest national importance and this information subsequently passed into the hands of the accused, Hurford. I must warn you that it is unlikely she acted alone in this perfidious work. Investigations are continuing and it is only a question of time before at least one more accomplice in this same department is named and brought to trial."

Copies of Hurford's statement and of the confession supposed to have been made by the Russian woman were now produced by the Prosecutor and handed to the judges. The Prosecutor declared: "It is not intended that these statements will be made public, as they refer in places to matters which will be dealt with in the closed sessions of this trial. Nevertheless, they form the basis of my examination of the two prisoners and I submit therefore that the Citizen Judges should have time to study them."

The Judge President accepted this submission and the trial was adjourned until the afternoon. Hurford and the woman Vanovitch were taken separately to detention rooms below the hall. The meal he was given there while the court was in recession was far better than anything served to him in the Lubianka; veal cutlets and potatoes with white bread, a piece of strong cheese and tea. He felt, illogically, that this was not an encouraging omen.

Back in court, the Prosecutor began immediately to cross-examine him.

"Are you a lecturer at the British Institute in Moscow?"

"Yes."

"And were you once an officer in the Intelligence Corps of the British Army?"

"Yes."

"Will you tell the Citizen Judges under what circumstances you came to be employed by the British Institute?"

"It was an arrangement made by British Intelligence so that I could work for them here." Hurford gave his answers as firmly as he could. He had rehearsed the whole cross-examination three times with the Assistant Prosecutor, repeating the answers they had prepared for him. He had been warned that if he deviated from the arranged pattern in any way, the microphone in front of him would be instantly switched off and the court cleared.

"And what operations did you carry out for your Intelligence chiefs?"

"I collected information and passed it back to them in London."

"Please repeat the answer more loudly."

Hurford did as the Prosecutor asked. He felt sick. His hands were shaking through nervousness and he gripped the rail at the front of the dock to steady them. He felt certain that the microphone was picking up his frenzied heartbeats and relaying them magnified through the hall. The faces of the spectators stared at him, malevolently it seemed, distorted with their hatred. To escape their hostility he wanted to throw himself on the floor and hide his face. You've got to hang on, he told himself agitatedly.

"Describe to the Citizen Judges how you received this information."

Steadily, under the guidance of the Prosecutor, Hurford worked his way through the confiteor of his offences; how a programme had been left on his seat at the Bolshoi; how negatives had been placed in the pocket of his raincoat at the Peking Hotel, where he had found microdots in books and the dead drops that had been used for other packages.

The cross-examination lasted for almost two hours and during the whole of that time the journalists from the West were taking notes. They had been scarcely able to hear his first answers, but as the authorities grew more confident that he would stick to the rehearsed script, the volume of the loudspeakers in the relay system was turned up. This was too good a story, too complete a performance, to be wasted.

When the last question had been answered, Hurford knew he was on the point of collapse. He asked the guard behind him for water and was handed a glass which the prison doctor had told him would contain a bromide to steady his nerves Now that the ordeal was over, he was no longer interested. The result of the trial and the sentence he would be given seemed unimportant. All he needed was the seclusion of his cell.

After cross-examining the Englishman, the Prosecutor turned his attention to Valentina Vanovitch. His examination of her was brief, almost derisory.

"Do you admit to copying certain documents taken from the files of your department on several occasions?"

"Yes."

"What were these documents?"

"Classified documents of a highly secret nature."

"Information that would have been useful to enemies of the Soviet Union?"

"Yes."

"And how did you copy them?"

"Sometimes on my typewriter. More often, because it was quicker, I used the photo-copying machine."

"Did you know that these documents would be passed over to British Intelligence?"

Momentarily the woman appeared to hesitate. Then, like a nervous swimmer forced to dive into forbidding waters, she steeled herself to answer "Yes."

Next the Prosecutor called his witnesses. Their testimony, he said, would prove that the accused were not being condemned on their confessions alone. Several witnesses were called to testify against Hurford: a waiter who claimed to have seen him at the Peking Hotel, the librarian from the Lenin Library who had issued him with books on cybernetics, Savarin who had discovered and identified the microdots on his letter to Noddick.

The evidence against Valentina Vanovitch was more slender. A girl from her office said that she had observed her typing furtively during the lunch break and two of her colleagues described her behaviour in the department as secretive and guilty. A woman who had shared an apartment with her for six years, said that recently she had been spending more money than she could possibly have saved from her salary and that she had been receiving lavish gifts from a man friend.

The last witness was a small man with Georgian features and a Georgian accent. He wore a red and grey check shirt, open-necked, with his shiny grey suit.

"What is your occupation?" the Prosecutor asked him.

"I am an instrument mechanic."

"And is it true that you work at the department where the accused

Valentina Vanovitch is employed?"

"Yes. There and in several other government departments. I am on the staff of the Central Maintenance Department for government offices. My job is to service photo-copying machines and other instruments."

"How often do you visit the office where the accused works?"

"Regularly once a month to service all their machines. Also whenever there is mechanical trouble, I am sent for."

"In a voluntary statement to the police, you said you had seen the accused in the photo-copying section at her offices."

"Yes. On two or three occasions when I arrived to service the machines, I found her in the room."

"And was it part of her duties to use this equipment?"

"No. There were only two people authorised to use any of the machines. The chief of the copying section and her assistant."

"I see. And on the occasions when

you found the accused there, did she give you any explanation for her presence in the room?"

"No. But she holds an important position in the department. She would not feel that she had to answer to me."

"In your opinion had she been using any of the equipment?"

"Yes," the man in the check shirt replied at once. "The photo-copier."

"How could you be so certain?"

"I could tell it had just been switched off, for the machine was still warm."

"Are you saying that the accused, Valentina Vanovitch, switched the machine off when she heard you coming?"

"Yes."

The spectators in the hall murmured in unison, a murmur that was both indignant and satisfied. They were not interested in the niceties of law. Here was evidence enough of the prisoner's guilt, even though the Prosecutor had led the witness to a conclusion and then passed if off as fact.

"That concludes the evidence which I am allowed to present in open court," the Prosecutor told the judges. "The next part of our case concerns the nature of the information which the two prisoners stole and since this affects the security of the state, I must ask that the court is cleared."

"In that case," the Judge President replied, "as it is already late, we will terminate these proceedings for today. The court will resume at ten o'clock tomorrow morning, when members of the public and the press will not be admitted."

Hurford was driven back to the Lubianka in a closed van. A small crowd had gathered outside the entrance to the court building and there was a mild demonstration as two guards led him out to the waiting vehicle. He heard booing and a few shouts of 'Capitalist spy' and 'Fascist dog'.

Back in his cell, he was visited by the prison doctor who told him:

"They tell me you behaved in an exemplary manner. Congratulations! The Prosecutor is extremely pleased with you."

"I feel terrible," Hurford complained. "Can't you do anything for my nerves?"

"I'll give you a sedative. You must have a good night's sleep."

The doctor gave him two pills which he swallowed without question. All he wanted was relief from the crushing depression and anxiety which were slowly destroying him. Even poison, a lethal draught and an instant's agony, he would have welcomed if it brought peace and a comforting void.

As it was, the night was one of deep but exhausting sleep. He woke next morning calmer, but feeling that all his reserves of willpower and all his energy were utterly drained. I'll never last the day out, he thought.

Back in court, the great hall empty of spectators was stripped of its dignity but not of its power. A scene enacted in the echoing silence was no longer drama, but ritual; speeches and questions were only a form of words, incantations before the final sacrifice.

Besides the judges, defending counsel and the two prisoners, two rows of top-ranking Soviet officials were present, seated at the front of the hall. Some of them Hurford had seen at diplomatic receptions: members of the Central Committee of the Communist Party, the chiefs of important ministries. They were waiting in their seats, severe and silent, when the prisoners were led into the hall. None of them, so far as Hurford could remember, had been present at the trial on the previous day.

Seeing this parade of political power, he felt a sudden tremor of fear. The whole atmosphere of the trial was different now. Instead of an elaborate piece of propaganda, it had become something grimly serious and, for that reason, sinister.

The Prosecutor stood up beside his table. There was a perceptible change in his bearing, a touch more arrogance, as though he were aware of his audience.

"Today we propose to bring another prisoner before you," he told the judges. "A man who is inextricably involved in the offences of the British spy Hurford, and who was responsible for the corruption of the other prisoner Valentina Vanovitch."

From the door at the side of the hall two soldiers led in an old man in army uniform. None of the political giants in the front rows of seats turned to look, but stared ahead with disciplined hostility.

The Prosecutor, ring-master at the circus of destruction, announced: "The prisoner before the court is Marshal Ivor Godotsky, Director General of the K.G.B."

33

HURFORD recognised Godotsky as the old man whom he had been taken to see through a spyhole in a cell at the Lubianka. Now that he had heard his name, he remembered seeing photographs of the Marshal in newspapers years before at the height of his military career. The man was so changed, aged prematurely, that he scarcely recognised him. In the prisoners' pen he sat erect, his soldier's instincts still stronger than the shame and despair that lined his face.

"You see here," the Prosecutor said scornfully, "a man who rose to one of the highest and most responsible positions in the Soviet; a man who has had every conceivable honour bestowed on him by a grateful country. For as a soldier he served that country well and his name is linked with some of the most glorious episodes in the history of revolutionary Russia. And yet you find him here today, flanked by a foreign spy and a shameful woman, guilty of the most dastardly crime a man can commit — treachery against his fatherland. Indeed it is only because the Soviet is generous, because she remembers those who serve her selflessly, that he did not appear before you and before the eyes of the world yesterday. The Supreme Council has decided to spare Godotsky — we can no longer honour him with the title of Marshal or even Comrade — the humiliation of a public trial."

Hurford glanced sideways at Godotsky, now seated in the middle of the dock between him and the Russian woman. That a man of the Marshal's record and importance had been working for the West must have been a shattering discovery for the highest echelons of Soviet power. He tried to imagine the impact in England if the Home Secretary had suddenly defected to the East. And Godotsky was potentially a much greater threat to security, because he would have access to all the information collected by Soviet Intelligence at home and throughout the world. No wonder Savage had been eager to exploit this Eldorado of secret knowledge.

The Prosecutor began to outline the case against Godotsky and the evidence, though mainly circumstantial, was damning. The Marshal had paid a private visit to the Bolshoi theatre with his assistant Valentina Vanovitch on the same evening as Hurford. He had lunched at the Peking Hotel on the day when photographic negatives of classified documents had been passed to the British spy. The librarian from the Lenin Library would testify that it was Godotsky, a keen student of cybernetics, who immediately before Hurford had borrowed the two books from which the incriminating microdots had been taken.

"Moreover," the Prosecutor stated, "I shall be able to show you that

Godotsky was almost the only man who had access to all the different information that Hurford sent back to London. By the admission of the Britisher, this included a list of the most important Soviet agents working in Britain. Then we know that at the Peking Hotel the photographs passed to him were of reports sent in by K.G.B. agents engaged in organising revolutionary activity at Portuguese universities. Finally we can exhibit the enlargements of the microdots found on Hurford's letter. These show intelligence reports from America and a list of students graduating from the K.G.B. training academy at Leningrad."

Events in other countries, subsequent to Hurford's arrival in Moscow, the Prosecutor went on to explain, indicated that a great deal of other information covering K.G.B. activities in all parts of the world had been passed to the intelligence services of Russia's enemies. As the judges knew, the K.G.B. was divided into several directorates each of which, for security reasons, worked strictly on its own. Even Heads of Directorates were allowed no more than a working knowledge of what went on elsewhere. Only two people had access to all the diverse documents and information that was known to have passed through Hurford's hands: Godotsky and his second-in-command, Kitimov. There was no shred of evidence against Kitimov. In fact it had been he who had put in train the investigation that had led to his chief's arrest.

"It could conceivably be argued that all this might be coincidence, however unlikely that may appear," the Prosecutor said. "But I have further evidence that will leave no doubt in your mind of the prisoner's guilt. Only two days after he was arrested, Godotsky was due to go abroad in a military delegation to Turkey. I shall call evidence to show he was planning to use this opportunity to leave Russia for ever. Perhaps he had already guessed that we had begun to have suspicions about his loyalty. Perhaps he could no longer resist the lure of all the money that was waiting for him outside Russia in payment for his services to the capitalist aggressors. We have reason to suppose that his mistress, the woman Vanovitch, would also have fled the country at the first opportunity so that together they would enjoy the shameful fruits of their treason."

Glancing at Godotsky, Hurford thought, Good God, the case against him is stronger than they have against me. He felt no sympathy for the renegade, only contempt.

To prove the case against this third prisoner, the Prosecutor next presented his evidence. First came a facsimile of a page from the ledgers of the Consolidated Balkan Bank.

It showed that twenty thousand pounds had been deposited anonymously to the account of one Ivan Garner. The second piece of evidence was a booking sheet from the Istanbul office of British

European Airways, which recorded a reservation in the name of I. Garner for flights from Istanbul to Rome and thence to Johannesburg.

"You will recall," the Prosecutor continued, "that in his statement the prisoner Hurford admitted that he had received instructions by radio to pick up a package from a dead-letter drop. You will recall too that he was arrested by the K.G.B. before he was able to carry out these instructions. When eventually he admitted this to us, two members of the security forces went to the dead-letter drop and searched the place. I now call one of the officers in question to testify."

The K.G.B. man who gave evidence looked stupid, tough and totally dedicated. He reminded Hurford of a Corsican who used to run a call-girl business from a café in Cannes. At the request of the Prosecutor he described how he had visited the dead-letter drop with one of his colleagues.

"And did you find a package there?"

"Yes."

"Was this the package?"

The K.G.B. man looked at a brown envelope which the Prosecutor held out to him. "Yes."

"Will you open the envelope, please, and show the court what it contains."

From the envelope the K.G.B. man pulled out what appeared to be a slim, dark book. One of the judges leant forward so that he could see it better. No one else in the hall showed any interest.

"What is that?"

"A passport."

"Indeed?" The Prosecutor took it from him with the nonchalance of an experienced conjuror. "A British passport to be precise. From it we learn that Her Britannic Majesty's Principal Secretary of State for Foreign Affairs requests us to allow the bearer to pass without let or hindrance. In other words he should be free to go where he likes. To Johannesburg, for example. And who is the bearer of this valuable document? It was issued in London to Ivan Garner, export manager, born in Poland but a naturalised British subject."

Holding up the open passport, the Prosecutor paused to make the most of this moment of drama.

"And who is Ivan Garner? From the photograph in the passport you will see that he is none other than Ivan Godotsky."

Part Four

Retouching

Retouching

34

AFTER landing at Tempelhof, the Russian plane taxied to the airport building and stopped. The passengers on a routine flight to East Germany had been told that there would be an unscheduled stop at Berlin, but nothing more. Looking back some of them may have noticed that the door at the rear of the aircraft was opened and the gangway steps lowered.

The two K.G.B. men who had been sitting with Hurford alone in the first-class compartment took him to the door. A hundred yards away across the tarmac three men stood waiting. One of them wore a fur hat and heavy black overcoat. The K.G.B. man on Hurford's left waved and there was a wave in reply from the waiting group.

"Off you go," the K.G.B. man told Hurford.

A moist spring sun was shining but the air still carried the bitterness of passing winter. Clutching his raglan topcoat to him as he walked down the steps, Hurford was conscious of the twenty-four pounds of weight that he had lost over the seven months he had spent in prison since his arrest. He felt physically feeble and wondered whether he could manage the walk across the tarmac without stopping to be sick.

The man in the fur hat, the Russian agent for whom he was being exchanged, walked towards him. As they passed each other, he looked at Hurford and smiled. Donaldson seemed thoroughly relaxed. He might have been a business-man setting out on a trip to a country where he knew he would be amusingly entertained.

In the shadow of the airport building the two other members of the waiting group shook Hurford by the hand. One wore B.E.A. uniform. The other, who introduced himself as Watson, did not have to explain that London had sent him. He had the same nondescript features, the same inconspicuous clothes, the same prosaic air of composure as all the men on Colonel Fenton's permanent staff.

"The plane's waiting." He nodded in the direction of a B.E.A. Viscount which stood at the far end of the airport building.

They entered the building and walked along a long corridor which ran the full length of it. Passengers, arriving and embarking, passed them on the way. Thin Americans in light-weight suits carrying grey attaché cases; German engineers from Dusseldorf and Stuttgart, fat and confident; middle-aged women with crimped hair clutching boarding cards, passports and travellers cheques in bony hands. Hurford, noticing that Watson glanced at him from time to time, realised that his nervous exhaustion must be showing itself. He clenched his hands in the pockets of his coat, determined to stick it out.

The B.E.A. officer left them at the

steps of the Viscount. There were two other passengers in the first-class compartment and they looked up irritably as Watson and Hurford went in. The plane had been delayed for twenty minutes on account of these two clowns.

When they were airborne, Hurford asked: "Any chance of a drink? I don't feel too hot."

"Did the Russians give you any pills before you left?"

"The doctor gave me a sedative, but it's wearing off now."

"Better not risk alcohol, then. I have something here which the M.O. in London gave me for you."

Watson held out two pills. Hurford felt inclined to refuse them. After what he had been through, he felt entitled to decide these matters for himself. But he had not the energy to make a protest. When lunch was served, he forced himself to drink a glass of tomato juice and eat half a bread roll.

"Better get some rest," Watson advised

him. "The reception at London Airport may be pretty nerve-racking."

"Reception? What reception?"

"We tried to keep it quiet, but the press have found out that you'll be on this plane."

The news filled Hurford with panic. So long as he had been engulfed in the womb of the Lubianka prison, he had not cared what the world might be saying about him. The thought that soon he would be produced, a political mongol child, to feed the curiosity of cameras and questions, revolted and alarmed him.

"What should I tell them?"

"Nothing. We'll rush you through. There'll be no press conference."

As the plane flew over Holland towards the North Sea, Hurford brooded over this piece of injustice. He had not even asked to return to England. Better fifteen years of prison with its comforting obscurity. When the Commissar of the Lubianka had told him he was to be exchanged for a Russian held at home, he had protested. He wanted to serve out his time, then find a job in some remote part of Russia, become absorbed and forgotten in the vast anonymity of 230 million people.

"Unfortunately," the Commissar had replied, "it is not for you or I to decide these matters. We are just a part of a much larger game."

He had said 'part' but he meant 'pawns' and he was right. Hurford knew he was merely a nameless piece of living matter, to be pushed one way or another in one of the numberless moves of the political game. He had no wish to return to England to be reviled or pitied, a failed spy. The prison Commissar had thought him a little mad and others would too.

Perhaps I am going mad, he told himself, remember the men who came back from Japan in the last war after three years in the bag, right round the bend.

The idea, like almost any other that

fell into his brain, took root instantly and flowered like a grotesque tropical plant for a few colourful moments. At once he was convinced that he was insane. They would be waiting for him at London, the doctors with their syringes, the male nurses with their strait-jackets.

He knew he had to find a way to cheat them and the answer was suicide. This idea too became immediately attractive. Better to die than live gibbering in an asylum. Slowly he worked out a plan.

Not far from where they were sitting, there was an emergency escape hatch, a window easy to knock out once the red handle had been pulled. First he must trick Watson, so the fellow would have no suspicions. He would get up and go to the toilet behind them. On the way back, while Watson's attention was still engrossed in his newspaper, Hurford would make a quick dive for the hatch. In seconds it would be over and he would be floating down from twenty-five thousand feet, drifting into unconsciousness before impact.

"I'm going out for a leak," he announced calmly, keeping the excitement out of his voice.

In the toilet he washed his hands and face and dabbed eau-de-cologne around his temples from the bottle provided. It was supposed to make one cool. Should he pray? On the whole he decided not. Suicide was mortal sin. Instead he counted up to twenty to steady his nerves and slipped back the catch on the door.

Watson was standing outside. He said: "I thought you might be feeling sick, so I came to see if there was anything I could do." His tone was suitably concerned but his level stare told Hurford that he had guessed his intentions. "I'm fine."

"Let's get back to our seats, then. We might ask the hostess for some more coffee."

An hour later the aircraft was making a long approach over London. Hurford recognised the Serpentine, the Carlton Tower Hotel, Lots Road power station and Kew Gardens. The pills Watson had given him appeared to have taken effect for he felt much calmer, his depression dwindling.

When the plane stopped, he looked out and saw Savage climb out of a waiting car. He was wearing a precisely tailored blue overcoat and a bowler. About a dozen journalists stood nearby in small groups and a television crew was waiting by its mobile camera. The other passengers watched as Watson and Hurford were allowed down the steps first. That evening they would be boasting in the pubs, "I was on the same plane as that lecturer chap. Suppose the Russians framed him just so they could get one of their own agents back."

Hurford wanted to turn round and tell them the truth; that he had been sent to spy and failed; that the whole business was futile and degrading. At the bottom of the steps the journalists crowded round as Watson tried to elbow a way through for both of them.

"Have you any statement to make, sir?"

"Are you glad to be back home?"

"Were you in fact working for British Intelligence?"

"No statements just now," Watson said firmly.

"How did the Russians treat you?"

Hurford was determined that no one was going to gag him. To hell with Savage. He told the journalists: "I've absolutely no complaints. None at all."

Watson pulled him through the crowd and into the car. By this time Savage was already sitting inside. He had taken off his bowler and was balancing it on his knees. As always he had an air of having the situation entirely under control.

"Nice to have you back, old chap."

"Why the hell can't I speak to those journalists?" Perversely, fear of the Press had been replaced by stubborn resentment.

"Later, Mike. We've got to pick those brains of yours first." Hurford sat back, determined he would tell them nothing. Why, after all those weeks of relentless interrogation, should he be faced with more questions? But on the way into London Savage asked him nothing. Instead he chatted in the flippant, self-deprecating style which made his conversation appear more intelligent than it was and so flattered the listener.

Leaving the main road at the Chiswick flyover, the driver took the car through Shepherd's Bush and Holland Park, before turning north. Hurford realised then that they were not taking him to London headquarters.

"I thought you wanted to question me?"

"Not before the M.O. has seen you. We're terribly modern these days. Blood tests, pep pills, douches, the lot."

"Where are you taking me now?"

"To our private place in Hampstead."

The doctor who was waiting for Hurford at the nursing home was Zollick, the man who had given him a medical examination before his appointment to the Institute. He made disparaging noises as he tested heart, chest, blood pressure and took samples of urine and blood.

"How long did you say you were in their hands?" he asked and when Hurford told him commented: "I would scarcely have believed it possible to do all this to a man in that time."

"What's the matter with me?"

"In the normal way you'd need at least a year's rest and nursing care. Even then there would be little chance of your ever being a hundred-per-cent fit again. But don't look alarmed! We've got a new wonder drug that will put you right."

"I've had enough of drugs," Hurford protested.

"Too much," Zollick agreed. "But if you ever want to get back to normal you'll take the treatment I prescribe."

"And what is that?"

"We'll keep you here for about three weeks. The treatment will start immediately the lab. sends back the results of certain tests I shall make."

So it was to be an asylum after all, Hurford thought. The chat about wonder drugs and three weeks didn't fool him. His first impulse was to refuse and demand his freedom, but suddenly freedom no longer had any appeal.

"Will I be alone?" he asked Zollick.

"Naturally. In a private room. You need complete rest and seclusion."

Seclusion was exactly what Hurford wanted. Solitary confinement which would give him a refuge from all the pressures that ranged about him, safety from the conspiracies that were being contrived, time to think out all the ideas which assailed his tired mind.

"Take me to my cell," he said.

35

PEOPLE who saw Savage's office
found difficulty in believing that
it was in the same building and
accountable to the same government
department as Colonel Fenton's austere
room. Fenton's walls were painted in
the uniform dirty cream of Whitehall,
but Savage had somehow tricked the
Ministry of Works into papering his
with regency stripes. He had jettisoned
the standard issue plywood-topped
desk and metal filing cabinet and
installed pieces intended for official
entertaining rooms in Downing Street
and Lancaster House. As a garnish he
had added various trophies won during
his career; a small Epstein sketch for
the bust of Gertrude Stein, an inlaid
box now used for cigarettes that had
once been prized by the head of the
Union Corse, a pair of porcelain vases

commissioned and then rejected by Guggenheim, a carved jade head of singular ugliness from Macao which the Portuguese Government still believed it had presented to General McArthur.

"What happens now?" Hurford asked, putting down his empty coffee cup.

"Three months leave on full pay. You need and deserve it."

"I feel fine." After a month under the care of Zollick, Hurford had been discharged and it was true that he felt immeasurably better. Besides putting on fifteen pounds in weight, he was eating and sleeping well. His nervousness and depression had disappeared almost miraculously, leaving him relaxed.

"Even so, a spell of leave will do you good."

"And afterwards?"

"Now that your face has been flashed on the world's goggle-box, we can never again use you operationally, I'm afraid. But there'll be a job falling free in the Bureau before your leave expires."

"Desk work? I doubt if that would suit me."

"Well, if you preferred to pull out, I could arrange a pretty handsome gratuity."

"That's very generous for a man who failed you." Hurford spoke without bitterness or sarcasm. The ordeal he had undergone in Russia now seemed a century away, and he no longer felt any resentment towards Savage or anyone else in London.

"Failed us?" Savage stopped spooning the remains of the sugar in his cup and looked incredulous. "You can't be serious!"

"You don't have to be magnanimous. I know I fouled it up."

Before replying, Savage got up from his desk, crossed the room and straightened the Epstein sketch, which was at least one-sixteenth of an inch out of true. The question had not embarrassed him in any way, but he was aware that he must plan what he answered. Carelessness often made people say things which they subsequently regretted but could not withdraw, and he wished to keep Hurford's friendship.

"I'm not one for hyperbole, as you well know, Mike. But this was possibly the greatest intelligence coup of all time."

"Coup? What do you mean?"

"Just think what we achieved. It's no exaggeration to say that the whole organisation of the K.G.B. has been shattered. In this country we picked up, tried and convicted six of their best agents and America, France, Belgium and West Germany did the same on our information. We could have brought in the lot here, if it hadn't been for the expense of trying and jailing them. Besides, think of the public alarm if we arrested four hundred and sixty Russian agents in Britain." This idea appeared to amuse Savage and he laughed, shaking his head "The Russians can only try to guess how much we know and they're badly shaken. The whole K.G.B. is being reorganised and all the top men have already been replaced."

"But thanks to me you've lost the source of your information. Godotsky and the woman are finished."

"My dear Mike, Godotsky wasn't working for us. As the Yanks would say, he was just the fall guy."

"Are you saying he wasn't guilty? He never denied the charges at the trial."

"No. He did a deal with the Prosecutor to protect his family. They had enough evidence to convict him twice over, anyway. So although Godotsky didn't confess to spying, he didn't deny it either. In return they agreed not to shoot him and to leave his family their freedom. It suited the Russians. A public trial for Godotsky would have meant a scandal at home and a propaganda defeat abroad. So he's running a canning factory in Siberia now, a life prisoner to all intents and purposes."

At first Hurford did not believe him. The story was an elaborate invention, designed to spare his feelings, to make him feel that his mission had not after all been a fiasco. Then he remembered an incident during the war, when a soldier had been brought before Savage charged with a piece of well-intentioned stupidity that had nearly cost a dozen lives. Savage was not the man to compromise with failure for sentiment or friendship.

"Then what about the woman, Vanovitch?" Hurford asked.

"It seems she really was having an affair with the old man. That was a thing we hadn't been counting on. After a few days' pressure she agreed to carry the can and save Godotsky from the firing squad. Once he had been arrested she knew she was finished. Russians are realists if nothing else."

Hurford understood what he meant. "But are you saying that neither of them had been working for us?"

"What an idea! They'd be far too expensive and far too dangerous."

"Then what about all that evidence

357

which was produced in court?"

"It was all planted. The documents and other bits and pieces had already reached us through our regular source. We used them to incriminate Godotsky. That was your job."

Since the days of his first interrogation at the Lubianka, Hurford had suspected that the real object of his assignment in Moscow was more complex than it appeared. The truth astounded him. He had never imagined that the plot could have been so devious and his part in it so insignificant.

"So I never sent you anything of value. I was nothing more than a sophisticated decoy."

"Nothing more? Believe me, your role was crucial and you played it bloody well."

"But why on earth didn't you tell me all this at the beginning?"

"Don't you see? You couldn't be told. Otherwise the Russians would have learnt the truth when they brainwashed you. If we wanted to deceive them we had to deceive you too."

In an instant Hurford saw the whole truth but was too appalled to accept it. "But this means you knew I'd be picked up by the K.G.B.!"

"Of course. It was one of our men who tipped them off."

"Are you saying that you sent me into that bloody business deliberately? The interrogation and the brain-washing and the drugs?" Hurford felt a rage begin to grip him. "Who the hell do you and Fenton think you are?"

"It was our plan, but the decision to use it was taken at the highest political level."

"I don't care a shit who took the decision. You had no right to do it without my consent. An experience like that could affect a man permanently."

"Don't get steamed up, Mike." Savage smiled at him in the engaging way he reserved for difficult opponents. "It's all over now and I can tell you we would never have dreamt of putting you into Russia if we had not got M.X.5."

"What the hell's that?"

"The drug with which Zollick has been treating you for the past month. It's the complete cure for anything the Communists could do to you; eradicates all the mental and physical after-effects. Long before we even approached you the drug had been tested and proved. We knew it would have you back to normal and a hundred-per-cent fit in no time at all."

His assurances did not assuage Hurford's indignation. It was he and not some vote-catcher in Westminster who had suffered in the Lubianka. He tried to relive the humiliation, the fear of death by execution and the excruciating agony of those hours in the Conveyor. But already the experience seemed remote and unreal.

Savage went on: "Look at it this way. You may have given us a year of your life, but you've done the country a service of incalculable value."

"Yes, a year of my life wasn't worth

much," Hurford remarked sarcastically, although he knew this was true.

"Was it worth fifteen thousand? Because that's what the Treasury have authorised me to pay you, if you decide to leave us."

Hurford shook his head in resignation. "As usual, you win."

"I think it's a fair payment. You can have a job with us for life or be back where you were before with fifteen grand in the bank; we could even see that you got your old job back."

"No thanks. That part of my life is over."

The real reason why he did not intend to return to Cannes was that Margery and he were going to live together again. She had been to visit him several times in the nursing home. When she had said: "Mike, darling, couldn't we have another try? I've changed a lot I promise you," he had agreed. At the time it had seemed a good idea and it still did, but he could not find the words to tell Savage. What reasons could he give? Because she had stood by him? The lame cliché was too typical of their relationship and he felt, superstitiously, that to use it might set them off to a bad start.

When he was about to leave he said to Savage: "You may have protected your real source in Russia by implicating Godotsky, but you've put an end to it as well. If all the top men in the K.G.B. have been axed, your man must have gone too."

"Don't worry about our source. It's still there and working." Even Savage could not restrain his self-satisfaction. "That's the beauty of the situation. The Russians are busy building up their whole intelligence network all over again and we know their every move."

They shook hands. Although it was agreed that Hurford should postpone any decision about his future until after his leave, they both knew his mind was already made up. The golden handshake, invested with his other savings, would give him a few hundred a year; enough as a basic income which he could supplement with literary work, reviews and translation.

As he paused by the door Savage said: "And it's good to know that you and Margery are back together. I'm terribly pleased for both of you, Mike, really."

36

AFTER dinner they drank their coffee on the hotel terrace. In the gardens beneath them the palm fronds swayed gently in the lightest of breezes. On the other side of the bay the lights of Funchal stretched in a sprawling network up the black hills. Single dots of light that were cars crawled slowly up impossibly steep, winding streets. In a village near the mountain peaks they were holding a fiesta and fireworks burst like distant gunfire. The siren of a cruise liner in the harbour boomed once, echoing in the mountains, calling passengers back from the bars and the casino.

"This really is a fabulous hotel," Margery said.

Agreeing, Hurford found himself at the same time wondering whether there was a hidden criticism in her remark.

He had chosen another hotel in the town because he thought it might be gayer, more to Margery's taste. But after a drink in its deserted black leather and white marble bar, they had decided to spend their first evening at Reid's.

In the bar behind them the band began to play; a tune popular soon after the war in an arrangement that made only the barest concessions to modern style. During the last half-a-dozen years Hurford had danced seldom and then only in French discotheques. But this was their sort of music, he reflected with a twinge of self-reproach; two people moving towards fifty and away from the trend.

To prove this to himself, he asked Margery to dance. There used to be a time when he found her dancing sensual to the point of being provocative and was jealous that other men might do the same. Now, although he could feel her thighs pressed against his own, there was no response. After a time, when she placed both arms round his neck and pulled his face into her hair, he felt no passion, only embarrassment.

"Mike, this is wonderful! Things can never go wrong for us again."

Her words and the sentiment sounded false. Not false, foreign, he told himself. It was he who was out of tune. He had broken away from their pattern of life, lived with a girl not much more than half his age, an ageing exile trying to remain young and bohemian. The gulf between Margery and him was of his making and it was he who would have to make the effort and grow accustomed once more to her conventions.

Everything will be all right when we're alone, he reassured himself, meaning when they were in bed. This would be the first night they had spent together since their marriage had crumbled. After he had left Zollick's nursing home, Margery had wanted him to go down to Camberley but he found two reasons for procrastinating.

First business matters to be arranged in London and then he had visited his father in Chesterfield. So their reunion, the coming together, had been at London Airport that morning. Hurford knew it would be better that way. Camberley was the Army and the Army hung over their relationship, a sword of dishonour.

They drank a bottle of Pol Roger and danced three times more and then walked back from Reid's to their hotel. Crossing the bridge over the ravine, their footsteps on the pebble-stone pavement were drumbeats over the rustle of crickets in the banana leaves.

He stripped as far as his underclothes and went into the bathroom with his pyjamas. When he came back into the bedroom she was already in bed and naked. Memories of certain occasions in the past and the effects of the champagne excited him as she pulled him, more gently than she used to, towards her. Astonishingly, she had managed to preserve the firmness of her body.

The act, though hardly ecstatic, was not the nervous fiasco he had feared. Afterwards she cried a little, through joy one supposed, and he fell asleep.

An hour later she woke him. This time her self-restraint had been abandoned. She's past forty, he thought, and still insatiable. Fighting down distaste he did his utmost. For one unguarded moment he caught himself wondering why with Nicole sex had been so different.

"The sword!" Margery gasped. "Mike, Mike, put me to the sword!"

The words still sounded in his brain after it was over and he lay there, unable to sleep. He had first used the phrase years before, returning home a little drunk and amorous after a Mess party. Margery had seized on it, believing that it lent romance to her importuning.

The door to the balcony of their room was open. Hurford got out of bed quietly, went out and sat on one of the blue canvas chairs outside. The cruise liner had sailed, leaving the harbour silent. A great moon had risen on the far side of the headland and the dark water of the bay shimmered in its reflection. Instead of peace, he could detect in the night a restlessness, a nervous energy imprisoned and waiting to be freed.

He was a prisoner too. He knew that now. Leaving the Lubianka only to become imprisoned by the flesh, a captive to all the demands, emotional and physical, that Margery would make.

He had no one to blame but himself. Only indecision, a lack of resolution, had prevented him from turning away when Margery had come to him at the nursing home and from rejecting her suggestions. Years before, when he had first joined the Army, he had determination enough. Victims of his purposefulness used then to call him intolerant, inflexible, even ruthless. But somewhere along the road his will-power had eroded away.

No doubt the fault had always been there, he decided, a hidden flaw in his character. He imagined his personality as a piece of dark marble, its perfect surface concealing the inner weakness, so that at the first tap of the mason's hammer it fell apart. There had to be a flaw or else he would never have been sent to Russia. Savage had chosen him for two reasons: as a man who superficially had all the qualifications for a difficult assignment, but one who would fall quickly, but not too quickly, to pieces.

The realisation of this fact neither annoyed nor shamed him. Instead he laughed quietly, because he had a secret that Savage did not know. Nobody knew. But the power was there, ready waiting, to be used whenever he chose. All through history men had sought the secret of power; philosophers, tyrants, mystics, but it had eluded them. They had failed because the secret was so simple. Power was not an idea; power was not a purpose; power was an instrument, single, indivisible and absolute.

The discovery and his secret excited him. After sitting on the balcony for twenty minutes savouring the pleasure of them, he could restrain himself no longer. He knew that he must go and look at it once more, just look.

A small entrance hall separated their bedroom from the hotel corridor and their suitcases were still there, on the collapsible stands where the porter had placed them. Hurford went silently through the bedroom. That was one thing the Army had taught him, to move silently.

His suitcase was not quite empty. In the linen pocket at the back was a small oblong roll of cloth, an old yellow duster once used to polish shoes. Taking it out of the case, Hurford went back into the bedroom, sat in the armchair by the dressing table and placed the roll in his lap.

After time enough to enjoy the sensation of having it there, he unrolled the duster. Sufficient moonlight filtered through the blinds to show the object it had concealed. It was a paperknife, beautifully fashioned from Toledo steel in the shape of a sword almost twelve inches long, strong, wickedly sharp. Margery had bought it in Gibraltar, not in one of the cheap tourist shops but at an expensive jeweller's. It was the knife with which he had failed to kill Norris.

Nobody knew it was the knife because no one was in the room when he stabbed, with an upward swinging blow at the man's heart and only pierced his stomach. Even Norris could not have seen the blade, concealed as it had been beneath Hurford's coat. And Hurford had been clever enough to hide it immediately afterwards as well.

He looked at it affectionately. All these years the knife had lain in his old tin trunk in the attic at Chesterfield. When, after leaving the nursing home, he had visited his father, he had brought it away with him.

Margery stirred in her sleep and sighed. Would she wake him again in the early morning, lustful fingers busy in his groin?

Hurford remembered how she had taunted him when he had told her he had discovered she was sleeping with Norris. Eight times in one night she had boasted, sneering at his own inadequacy. He had not known whether to disbelieve her. The memory of her jibes no longer worried him and never would again, now that he had his secret.

He sat in the dark looking at the knife and thinking not of Margery nor of Norris but of power. Now that he had power to what end was he supposed to use it? He was so absorbed in this problem, that he scarcely noticed the light when it appeared.

At first it was tiny, no bigger than a will-o'-the-wisp in the corner of the room. Slowly it grew in size and luminosity. It had no shape that he could recognise, only intensity. When at last it spoke he knew it was the angel.

And the angel said unto him, take up thy sword and it shall set thee free. The walls of the prison will fall with a great sound when you raise the sword that is the sword of light.

Trembling and excited he picked up the knife. God had commanded him in the voice of the angel. He had been given the secret of power and now he was being told how to use it.

Margery was sleeping and he went to her, sword in hand. As he drove the point into her throat she gave a strangled gasp. Blood spouted in a jet and her body writhed convulsively. He held a pillow over her face until he knew she was dead.

Downstairs the night porter was making entries in his private cash book. Hurford asked him whether it would be possible to book a seat on the early morning plane to Lisbon.

"No possibility at all, Senhor. Only an hour ago I tried for another guest who has been called back to Paris urgently. The morning plane is fully booked and the waiting list closed."

Outside in the street two taxis were waiting. He took the first and made the driver drive him to the harbour. The cruise liner had sailed but two other ships were moored at the quay, one Greek, the other Portuguese. Near the Greek ship two sailors stood smoking and Hurford went up to them.

"When do you sail?" he asked.

"Tomorrow night."

"And that one?" He pointed towards the Portuguese steamer.

"The *Funchal*? She leaves for Lisbon at eleven tomorrow morning."

Eleven would be too late. The only chance would be to find a fisherman who would take him to Porto Santo or better still to the Canary Islands. A man in a water-front bar advised him, after a couple of drinks, to try a small beach two miles along the coast.

The taxi-driver took him there and he walked down a steep, winding path to a cluster of huts and a small café. The fisherman he spoke to was slow of understanding and explanations were tedious. The man, realising he must be in trouble, pushed his price up to five thousand escudos. Hurford offered him eight hundred in notes, all he had left of twenty-five pounds he had changed when they had arrived on the island.

"When do I get the rest?"

"As soon as I can cash some travellers cheques at the other end."

"No. You must pay before we sail. Your hotel will cash the cheques."

Walking back to Funchal, he laughed, recognising destiny. He was a prisoner on the island, escaping from one kind of captivity into another. If they had gone to Venice as Margery had suggested, things would have been different.

There was only one escape; a leap off any of the sheer cliffs to the rocks below, but he spurned self-destruction. What was the alternative? Arrest, trial

376

and years in a Portuguese prison.

He remembered the Lubianka with its damp walls. In the long hours of silence there had been peace and contentment. The truth exploded in his mind with a brilliance more dazzling than all the fireworks in Madeira. Prison was what he longed for, the cool comfort of stone, the serenity of solitude.

At the hotel the night porter, his accounts finished, dozed over a newspaper. Hurford shook him gently.

"Call the police," he said. "I've murdered my wife."

37

AT the K.G.B. headquarters Claudia Auer opened the metal cupboard in the photo-copying room and began checking stock. The new security regulations meant extra work for her. Every sheet of copying paper, all the chemicals, had to be checked once a week and accounted for. No member of headquarters staff was allowed to even enter the room, except for her and her assistant.

When she had almost finished, a man in a grey suit and red and grey check shirt came into the room. She recognised him as the instrument mechanic from the Central Maintenance Department.

"Good morning, Citizen. I have come to carry out the monthly service of your machines."

"Very well."

She took no notice of him as he went about his work. Having unplugged one of the two copying machines, he loosened four screws and lifted up the lid. The checking and oiling of the moving parts were routine work, easily accomplished and there was another simple job for him to do.

Inside the lid of the machine there had been fixed a tiny camera of British manufacture. It was not more than half the size of a matchbox, with a lens that was one of the smallest ever developed, equal in diameter to a decent sized needle. The camera was fully automatic, its winding mechanism and shutter actuated by a photo-electric cell every time the copying machine was used. It was an instrument that the mechanic admired enormously and loved to handle, a masterpiece of miniaturisation. Without removing it, he flipped open the back and took out a minute roll of exposed film which he slipped into his pocket. Then he recharged the camera and replaced the lid of the copying machine.

The second copying machine and the microdot enlarger both contained similar cameras, which he unloaded and replenished while servicing the machines. That gave him three rolls of film with a duplicate of every document that had been copied, every microdot that had been enlarged in the room during the past month. By the time he had finished, Claudia Auer had completed her stocktaking and left the room. This gave him plenty of time to slide the three rolls into a dummy cigarette which he concealed in a half empty packet. Then, with the cigarettes in his breast pocket and his bag of tools under his arm he left the building.

That evening there was to be a demonstration outside the British Embassy. As a good party member he had volunteered for the duty of standing outside the gates and shouting slogans. A few missiles would of course be thrown at the windows; several stones, some rotten fruit and at least one crumpled cigarette packet.

THE END

A FOOT IN THE GRAVE
Bruce Marshall

About to be imprisoned and tortured in Buenos Aires, John Smith escapes, only to become involved in an aeroplane hijacking.

DEAD TROUBLE
Martin Carroll

Trespassing brought Jennifer Denning more than she bargained for. She was totally unprepared for the violence which was to lie in her path.

HOURS TO KILL
Ursula Curtiss

Margaret went to New Mexico to look after her sick sister's rented house and felt a sharp edge of fear when the absent landlady arrived.

THE DEATH OF ABBE DIDIER
Richard Grayson

Inspector Gautier of the Sûreté investigates three crimes which are strangely connected.

NIGHTMARE TIME
Hugh Pentecost

Have the missing major and his wife met with foul play somewhere in the Beaumont Hotel, or is their disappearance a carefully planned step in an act of treason?

BLOOD WILL OUT
Margaret Carr

Why was the manor house so oddly familiar to Elinor Howard? Who would have guessed that a Sunday School outing could lead to murder?

THE DRACULA MURDERS
Philip Daniels

The Horror Ball was interrupted by a spectral figure who warned the merrymakers they were tampering with the unknown.

THE LADIES
OF LAMBTON GREEN
Liza Shepherd

Why did murdered Robin Colquhoun's picture pose such a threat to the ladies of Lambton Green?

CARNABY
AND THE GAOLBREAKERS
Peter N. Walker

Detective Sergeant James Aloysius Carnaby-King is sent to prison as bait. When he joins in an escape he is thrown headfirst into a vicious murder hunt.

MUD IN HIS EYE
Gerald Hammond

The harbourmaster's body is found mangled beneath Major Smyle's yacht. What is the sinister significance of the illicit oysters?

THE SCAVENGERS
Bill Knox

Among the masses of struggling fish in the *Tecta*'s nets was a larger, darker, ominously motionless form . . . the body of a skin diver.

DEATH IN ARCADY
Stella Phillips

Detective Inspector Matthew Furnival works unofficially with the local police when a brutal murder takes place in a caravan camp.

STORM CENTRE
Douglas Clark

Detective Chief Superintendent Masters, temporarily lecturing in a police staff college, finds there's more to the job than a few weeks relaxation in a rural setting.

THE MANUSCRIPT MURDERS
Roy Harley Lewis

Antiquarian bookseller Matthew Coll, acquires a rare 16th century manuscript. But when the Dutch professor who had discovered the journal is murdered, Coll begins to doubt its authenticity.

SHARENDEL
Margaret Carr

Ruth didn't want all that money. And she didn't want Aunt Cass to die. But at Sharendel things looked different. She began to wonder if she had a split personality.

MURDER TO BURN
Laurie Mantell

Sergeants Steven Arrow and Lance Brendon, of the New Zealand police force, come upon a woman's body in the water. When the dead woman is identified they begin to realise that they are investigating a complex fraud.

YOU CAN HELP ME
Maisie Birmingham

Whilst running the Citizens' Advice Bureau, Kate Weatherley is attacked with no apparent motive. Then the body of one of her clients is found in her room.

DAGGERS DRAWN
Margaret Carr

Stacey Manston was the kind of girl who could take most things in her stride, but three murders were something different . . .

THE MONTMARTRE MURDERS
Richard Grayson

Inspector Gautier of Sûreté investigates the disappearance of artist Théo, the heir to a fortune.

GRIZZLY TRAIL
Gwen Moffat

Miss Pink, alone in the Rockies, helps in a search for missing hikers, solves two cruel murders and has the most terrifying experience of her life when she meets a grizzly bear!

BLINDMAN'S BLUFF
Margaret Carr

Kate Deverill had considered suicide. It was one way out — and preferable to being murdered.

BEGOTTEN MURDER
Martin Carroll

When Susan Phillips joined her aunt on a voyage of 12,000 miles from her home in Melbourne, she little knew their arrival would germinate the seeds of murder planted long ago.

WHO'S THE TARGET?
Margaret Carr

Three people whom Abby could identify as her parents' murderers wanted her dead, but she decided that maybe Jason could have been the target.

THE LOOSE SCREW
Gerald Hammond

After a motor smash, Beau Pepys and his cousin Jacqueline, her fiancé and dotty mother, suspect that someone had prearranged the death of their friend. But who, and why?

CASE WITH THREE HUSBANDS
Margaret Erskine

Was it a ghost of one of Rose Bonner's late husbands that gave her old Aunt Agatha such a terrible shock and then murdered her in her bed?

THE END OF THE RUNNING
Alan Evans

Lang continued to push the men and children on and on. Behind them were the men who were hunting them down, waiting for the first signs of exhaustion before they pounced.

CARNABY AND THE HIJACKERS
Peter N. Walker

When Commander Pigeon assigns Detective Sergeant Carnaby-King to prevent a raid on a bullion-carrying passenger train, he knows that there are traitors in high positions.

TREAD WARILY AT MIDNIGHT
Margaret Carr

If Joanna Morse hadn't been so hasty she wouldn't have been involved in the accident.

TOO BEAUTIFUL TO DIE
Martin Carroll

There was a grave in the churchyard to prove Elizabeth Weston was dead. Alive, she presented a problem. Dead, she could be forgotten. Then, in the eighth year of her death she came back. She was beautiful, but she had to die.

IN COLD PURSUIT
Ursula Curtiss

In Mexico, Mary and her cousin Jenny each encounter strange men, but neither of them realises that one of these men is obsessed with revenge and murder. But which one?

LITTLE DROPS OF BLOOD
Bill Knox

It might have been just another unfortunate road accident but a few little drops of blood pointed to murder.

GOSSIP TO THE GRAVE
Jonathan Burke

Jenny Clark invented Simon Sherborne because her daily gossip column was getting dull. Then Simon appeared at a party — in the flesh! And Jenny finds herself involved in murder.

HARRIET FAREWELL
Margaret Erskine

Wealthy Theodore Buckler had planned a magnificent Guy Fawkes Day celebration. He hadn't planned on murder.

SANCTUARY ISLE
Bill Knox

Chief Detective Inspector Colin Thane and Detective Inspector Phil Moss are sent to a bird sanctuary off the coast of Argyll to investigate the murder of the warden.

THE SNOW ON THE BEN
Ian Stuart

Although on holiday in the Highlands, Chief Inspector Hamish MacLeod begins an investigation when a pistol shot shatters the quiet of his solitary morning walk.

HARD CONTRACT
Basil Copper

Private detective Mike Farraday is hired to obtain settlement of a debt from Minsky. But Minsky is killed before Mike can get to him. A spate of murders follows.